Michael Bartlett has been a professional writer for over 50 years. Much of his earlier work was for radio, television and the stage. He has been a regular writer for programmes such as *The Archers* (Radio 4), *Rainbow* (Thames TV) and *Jackanory* (BBC TV), and he has also written numerous original plays which have been staged for radio, TV and theatre across the UK. In the past few years he has been writing novels and short stories. He lives with his wife in Norfolk.

In memory of my mother, Doris Ilott (1915-2007) who taught me how to be a non-conformist.

"If a man does not keep pace with his companions, perhaps it is because he hears a different drummer. Let him step to the music which he hears, however measured or far away."

- Henry David Thoreau

Michael Bartlett

A DIFFERENT DRUM

A Collection of Short Stories

AUSTIN MACAULEY PUBLISHERS™
LONDON • CAMBRIDGE • NEW YORK • SHARJAH

Copyright © Michael Bartlett 2024

The right of Michael Bartlett to be identified as the author of this work has been asserted by the author in accordance with sections 77 and 78 of the Copyright, Designs and Patents Act 1988.

All rights reserved. No part of this publication may be reproduced, stored in a retrieval system, or transmitted in any form or by any means, electronic, mechanical, photocopying, recording, or otherwise, without the prior permission of the publishers.

Any person who commits any unauthorised act in relation to this publication may be liable to criminal prosecution and civil claims for damages.

This is a work of fiction. Names, characters, businesses, places, events, locales, and incidents are either the products of the author's imagination or used in a fictitious manner. Any resemblance to actual persons, living or dead, or actual events is purely coincidental.

A CIP catalogue record for this title is available from the British Library.

ISBN 9781035849246 (Paperback)
ISBN 9781035849253 (ePub e-book)

www.austinmacauley.com

First Published 2024
Austin Macauley Publishers Ltd®
1 Canada Square
Canary Wharf
London
E14 5AA

The author gratefully acknowledges the valuable assistance of Eric Barker and Dee Palmer in the preparation of this book.

Table of Contents

Learning Arabic	11
Just One of Those Days	30
That Was Lovely, Dear	41
Parking Mad	58
Snapshots	72
There's A Slight Depression Centred Over Britain	83
BR-Exit	110
The Blues in Black and White	121
The Reunion	128
The Day Granny's Vulture Had Hiccups	138

Learning Arabic

She was stupid. She knew she was stupid because everyone told her so, her father, her brother, her teachers.

"I don't see how anyone can be as dumb as you," said her father.

"Thicko," said her brother.

"The level of your stupidity is beyond belief," said her teacher.

Constantly being told she was stupid gave her very little incentive to prove them wrong. It was not made any easier by everyone assuming she was too stupid to spell her own name.

"There is only one 'e' in Angela," she was always told but the name on her birth certificate was Angeela owing to the fact that her father had been drunk when he went to register her birth. Not her fault but it became another stick to beat her with.

Growing up was not a happy process and the first few years at her senior school were no better. She had more or less become resigned to a miserable, lonely, stupid existence but then she met Sarah.

Sarah arrived during her third year at Gorman High School. She breezed into the classroom at the beginning of the spring term, fourteen years old and with self-confidence oozing out of her. Within days it seemed she'd been at the school for ever.

It was three weeks later during the lunch break that she first spoke to Sarah or rather Sarah spoke to her. She came up to Angeela where she stood, alone, in her usual corner of the playing field. Angeela flinched, expecting some cutting remark but Sarah surprised her.

"Hi. I'm Sarah. I see you're on your own. Mind if I join you."

Without waiting for an answer she leant back against the fence and surveyed the rest of the school milling about.

"You're Angeela, aren't you? Interesting name, rather pretty."

"No one else seems to think so."

"You don't want to take any notice of them. Look at them all, yap, yap, yapping away with nothing to say."

Angeela blinked. This wasn't the sort of conversation she was used to.

"I've been watching you and I see you're always on your own. Don't you have any friends?"

"No. They all think I'm stupid."

"More fool them. Well, now, we can be friends, can't we? I like people who aren't part of a large crowd."

Angeela didn't know what to say but after a moment she mumbled "I'd like that."

"Good. That's settled." Sarah paused. "Tell you what, I think Angeela is a very nice name but I can see it's caused you a few problems so why don't I call you Angie? What d'you think?"

And so it began. A friendship that changed her life.

Angeela, or Angie as she began to think of herself, was instinctively suspicious of any kindness and she took a while to settle into this sudden friendship. She was reluctant to let her guard down completely until one day an incident in school changed everything.

It was a Tuesday morning during a history lesson. Angie had been asked a question and had got it wrong. The teacher, who had been in a bad mood since the start of the lesson, was cutting.

"You stupid girl. Don't you know anything? I wonder why I waste my time trying to get anything into your thick skull."

Some of the other pupils started giggling and Angie was close to tears when suddenly Sarah stood up.

"That's despicable," she said, "I think you should apologise to Angie. You should never say someone is stupid, no one is naturally stupid, not even those giggling morons over there."

The teacher stood there, mouth agape as Sarah went on. "A good teacher would accept that and try and work out where a particular person's intelligence lies, not constantly put them down. You should be ashamed of yourself."

The teacher was incandescent with rage. The class was silent. Sarah was ordered out of the room. She did not reappear in class that day or the next but on Thursday there she was again as bright and sunny as ever.

Later, when Angie asked what had happened Sarah just shrugged. "Our Head of Year had a long chat with me and I was told to make myself scarce for a couple of days. No sweat."

Angie knew that wasn't the full story but clearly Sarah was not going to say anymore. She tried to say thank you but Sarah brushed it aside. "I can't stand injustice," she said.

"But I'm really not very bright."

"Nonsense. Get this, Angie, you are not stupid. There'll be something you can do better than other people. We just need to find it and then you've got to learn to have faith in yourself."

Angie thought this was easier said than done but Sarah was having none of it.

"You don't know what you can do until you try. That's how Hannibal got the elephants over the mountains."

"Who's Hannibal?"

"Carthaginian general back in the day. Took a herd of fighting elephants over the Alps and kicked seven kinds of shit out of the Romans. No one thought he could do it, but he did."

Sarah's confidence was infectious but for Angie, the climb to any degree of self-confidence was long and hard.

* * *

It was in their fifth year at school when Angie's *'Elephants over the Alps'* moment happened. It was the early days of teaching IT in schools and there were only a limited number of computers available to learn on. However, from the moment she first sat down at a keyboard with a screen in front of her Angie felt at home. It all seemed to come naturally to her.

Before long some of her classmates were starting to get rather basic machines at home and Sarah urged Angie to ask her parents for one. She did, but the only result was gales of laughter.

"You want a computer? Well, that would be a waste of money, wouldn't it? Don't suppose you'd even know how to turn it on."

When Angie relayed this conversation Sarah's mouth tightened. "Right then. Here's what we'll do. I'll get one myself."

"But you don't even like the IT lessons."

"No, but then you can come round mine and practise as much as you like. I have an instinct about this, Angie. I think you're a natural."

And she was. The moment her fingers touched the keyboard she seemed to become part of the machine. Before long people at school were asking her help with technical things they didn't understand.

She didn't like it. "I wish they wouldn't," she said to Sarah, "they're all so much cleverer than me. It's embarrassing."

"'Clever' is a relative term," said Sarah, "it means different things for different people."

"But I've always been laughed at. I don't know what to do when people ask me to help them."

"You help them," said Sarah, "self-belief, Angie, they believe you can help them, so you can."

Angie found the last few years at school much less stressful. Being obviously good at something made her life easier, but a lifetime of not having any self-confidence could not be shed overnight.

* * *

In the fullness of time Sarah went into the 6th form and then on to university while Angeela went to a technical college to study IT. By the time Sarah had graduated, Angie was working as a computer programmer for an insurance company but her sense of personal inferiority died hard.

"You've got to become independent," said Sarah and Angie, fed up with the constant contempt at home, agreed. With Sarah's help she moved into a little bed-sit and the whole pattern of her life changed.

Sarah got a job as an administrator with a big international consultancy firm and by her mid-twenties she was earning enough money to buy herself a smart bungalow on the edge of the town.

Angie's work was appreciated by her manager at the insurance company but her diffidence and obvious lack of self-confidence meant she was constantly passed over for promotion.

Sarah passed her driving test on the third attempt and bought herself a car.

Angie eventually gave in to Sarah's persuasion and also took driving lessons. "I don't know why I'm doing this," she said, "I'll never pass the test."

"Of course you will," said Sarah, "remember you can…"

"…do anything so long as I believe I can. Yes, I know," said Angie. "All right, Sarah, I'll give it a go."

She gave it a go. She passed first time.

* * *

After a few years Angie had saved enough money to move out of the bed-sit and into a small flat above an ironmonger's shop in the High Street. She never really developed a social life of her own but she met a number of Sarah's friends of both sexes and gradually learned to relax with them, especially as they all seemed to like her.

She spent a lot of time with Sarah. They did something together most weekends and often met during the week as well, sometimes for a drink, sometimes for a meal or they would get a take-away and share it in Angie's flat or Sarah's bungalow.

A few times they went on holiday together, usually with a couple of Sarah's other friends. They would rent a cottage, walk and swim and put the world to rights. Angie loved these trips, both the travelling and the fact that Sarah's friends accepted her naturally as one of them.

Before long they expanded their holidays by hiring a big camper van and travelling across Europe to France, to Spain, to Italy taking it in turns to drive.

* * *

And so life drifted on for some years. Eventually, spurred on by Sarah using the Hannibal mantra, Angie applied for another, better-paid job and, slightly to her surprise, she got it. Sarah was never triumphant on these occasions, just pleased for her friend.

One day Angie was wandering round the living room at the bungalow waiting for Sarah before they went out when she noticed a language teaching book open on Sarah's desk.

"Are you learning Arabic?" she asked Sarah when she appeared.

Sarah wrinkled her nose. "Well, sort of," she said.

Angie smiled. "I know. After our last holiday I bought a Spanish course with a book and a CD. Tried the first two lessons and now it just sits on the shelf."

"Good intentions, eh?" said Sarah and changed the subject.

Angie thought no more of it but then one evening as Sarah was preparing to leave Angie's flat and drive home she said out of the blue. "Oh, by the way, I won't be able to see you next week. I'm going away for ten days or so."

"Oh, anywhere nice?"

Sarah was vague. "Not really. Just something I've got to do."

She did not offer any more information and Angie didn't like to ask.

Over the next couple of years these unexplained trips continued every few months until Angie stopped thinking about them. It was just one of those things that Sarah did.

* * *

And so the years passed until they each reached their thirty-year milestone. Both women were still single. Angie was quite happy about this but her constant dread had always been that Sarah would meet someone and get married.

Once, greatly daring, Angie asked her about it. "Have you never thought about getting married, Sarah, settling down?"

Sarah laughed. "The last thing I want to do is settle down. I prefer to take things as they come. That's much more fun."

"But wouldn't you like a family, children?"

Angie herself had never wanted children but she knew most women did and she was certain that Sarah would make a wonderful mother.

Sarah's response to this question was unexpected. Her face went dark and there was a long pause before she said, "I have all the children I need, thank you."

She added nothing to this enigmatic comment and Angie didn't like to press it any further.

And then one day Angie suddenly received a phone call out of the blue.

"Angie, it's Sarah. Can you come over tonight?"

"Of course I can. Has anything happened?"

"Tell you when you get here."

On and off during the day Angie wondered what was happening. Had Sarah got a job abroad? Was she moving away from the area? Was she going to get married after all? Was she pregnant?

The truth, when they were sitting in Sarah's living room, each with a glass of wine in front of them, was far, far worse than anything she could have thought of.

"There's no easy way to say this, Angie, but I have cancer. A particularly nasty cancer."

Angie was numb. "But it can be treated? Right?"

"There is treatment, but at best they think it will only delay things. There's no cure, I'm afraid."

"Oh, Sarah, no."

Sarah leaned over and took Angie's hand. "Now then, Angeela, I need you to be strong."

Sarah only ever called her Angeela when she wanted to emphasise something so Angie swallowed and nodded.

"I may have a year, could be less, so there are things to sort out and for that I need your help."

"Me? But what can I do?"

"Quite a lot actually. First, I want you to be the executor of my will."

"Oh, I couldn't."

"Yes, you can. I'll explain exactly what I want done. The solicitor will do most of it but I want someone I can trust to keep an eye on things."

"But I'd be useless at…"

"Nonsense. You don't know what you can do until you try. Remember that's how Hannibal got the elephants over the mountains."

"Bugger Hannibal. I'm sick to death of that bloody man."

Sarah laughed. "That's better. You're much stronger when you get angry."

With an effort Angie controlled herself. "Well…in that case…Do I need to know what's in your will?"

"Of course, but I haven't actually written it yet. I'm sorting that out tomorrow. One thing I can tell you though. I'm leaving this bungalow to you."

Angie was dumbfounded. "But you can't."

"Why not?"

"It's too valuable."

"So what? I've got no family left and it's high time you got out of that tiny flat."

This was all too much and Angie burst into tears.

Sarah, being Sarah, planned everything meticulously and Angie, being Angie, was carried along on the positive tide as she had always been.

Sarah had said she might have a year. In reality, it was only seven months. At the end, Angie was with her in the hospice holding her hand. She suddenly felt it gripped tightly and then Sarah said, rather faintly, "Sorry about this, Angie…no please don't cry."

"Oh, Sarah…"

"Now listen to me. Remember what I've always said, you can do anything so long as you believe you can."

"But I can't do it without you."

"Yes, you can. Remember Hannibal. Call my solicitor, make sure everything is sorted out properly for me and get those bloody elephants over the Alps."

The funeral, and the meetings with the solicitor all passed in a blur but finally, Angie found herself installed in Sarah's bungalow – her new home.

She looked round this place where she had been so happy. It was full of so many familiar things but the one thing she wanted was no longer there. For a moment she wondered if she could bear to live there without Sarah but then it seemed a ghostly finger tapped her on the shoulder and she could almost hear Sarah's voice saying, "That's quite enough of that, Angeela. Come on, get on with it."

It was about two months later when there was a ring at the door bell one evening. When she answered it she saw a man, probably in his late thirties, with a light olive complexion. He had stepped back off the front step and was standing on the path.

He gave a slight bow. "Hallo, I am a friend of Sarah's. My name is Mahir. And you are Angeela, yes. Angie, I am right?"

She was very cautious. "Yes, but Sarah's not here."

"No, of course not. Sarah is very sadly dead. I saw you at her funeral."

"Did you? I didn't see you."

"No. I kept…how do you say…a low profile. I did not want to intrude."

She was still instinctively cautious with strangers. "Okay. So…what do you want?"

"First I want to give you this." He stepped forward and handed her an envelope. "It is from Sarah. Next, I realise this is big surprise so I will go and sit on your front wall so you can close the door and go inside and be safe while you read it."

For a moment she felt embarrassed as she realised what he must be thinking, but she took the envelope.

"Oh. Well. Thank you. Would you like anything? A glass of water?"

"Nothing, thank you. I wait while you read." He gave her a beaming smile, walked back down the path and sat on the wall looking out on the street.

Rather flustered she closed the door and went back into the living room. She ripped open the envelope and scanned the contents quickly – it was definitely Sarah's handwriting. She sat down and began reading.

Dear Angie,

I hope you are now living in the bungalow and are happy and comfortable. I have asked Mahir to wait a few weeks after you moved in before delivering this letter. He also had firm instructions about giving it to you and then retreating to give you time to read it in private and in what you probably think of as safety.

She had another moment of embarrassment then, thinking of the man sitting on her garden wall.

However, Mahir is a very dear friend and completely trustworthy so you have nothing to fear. Angie, I need to ask you to do something for me, something I can no longer do myself. I am asking you because of our long friendship and my knowledge – which I suspect you will initially deny – that you have the strength to carry it out.

Darling, Angie, you have no idea of the joy I've had being your friend, helping you here and there, encouraging you (with Hannibal's help) and watching you grow in confidence. And grow you have, though maybe there is still a way to go. If you do this thing for me, Angie, then I think you will be taking another step towards becoming the person I know you can be, in fact, the person I know you are even if you haven't realised it yet. I know how much you have always valued our friendship but, believe me, I have also valued it too. You have given me so much, Angie, you are a genuine person and genuine people are very rare.

Please listen to what Mahir has to say, he will explain everything. I will be so happy if you will help pick up the reins where I was forced to leave off. You are a much stronger person than you realise, Angie, and it has been a delight and a privilege to be your friend.

Love Sarah

It was too much. The letter fell to the floor and she burst into tears.

It was twenty minutes later when she suddenly remembered the man sitting on her garden wall. She dried her eyes, went to the door and called.

"Mahir, so sorry to keep you waiting. Please come in?"

He came towards her smiling. "Thank you. You are happy with Sarah's message, yes?"

"Yes, of course, I didn't mean to leave you out there so long."

"Not important."

"Sarah said she wants me to do something for her and that you will explain."

"Yes." He paused. "I may sit, please?"

"Oh, yes, yes, of course."

He sat down in one of the armchairs by the fireplace and then paused gathering his thoughts.

"Sarah, she talks about you very much. She admires you too."

"Admires me?"

"Yes, she says you are very strong but you don't always know it."

"Oh."

"So, Angeela, this is the situation."

He began to talk and as the import of what he was saying got through to her she went cold with fear.

Sarah had, apparently, been part of VolAid, a group of volunteer workers who sourced aid for Syrian refugees living in camps in Turkey. Many of these people had lost everything when they fled from Syria's civil war and now they were desperate for food, clothes, medicines, all the basics to stay alive. When they had assembled a full load volunteers drove a transit van across Europe to Turkey to deliver the supplies in person to make sure they reached the people who needed them. Once there, the volunteers would spend a few days helping families, especially those with children, before returning to the UK to gather more supplies.

"There were four of us on each journey. Sarah, myself and two others, Bella and Patrick. There were other vans, other teams but that was our group."

"All volunteers?"

"Yes, though some of us have particular skills. For example, I am Syrian but I am also an Emergency Care Assistant with the ambulance service and Bella is a qualified child nurse. Very useful. There are a lot of desperate children in these camps."

Realisation had gradually dawned on Angie. "And this is what you want me to do? Take Sarah's place?"

"Yes."

"But I couldn't. Me? Drive to Turkey. It's not possible."

"Sarah said you could do it."

"Yes, but Sarah's not here." She instantly regretted saying that. "Sorry, I didn't mean it quite like that."

"Do not worry. I understand."

She could not do this. It was impossible. She still felt uneasy walking into a pub on her own. How the hell could she drive a van across Europe to Turkey?

She tried to explain this to Mahir but he just said.

"Yes, Sarah said this is how you would feel but she believed in you, Angeela. If she thought you could do it, then I know you can."

"All very well for you, mate," she thought, *"you haven't spent a lifetime being bullied and despised."*

He had been watching her closely and he suddenly smiled.

"I know what it is you are thinking, Angeela." He hesitated. "And I think I know how you are feeling. It is not nice when people look down on you and treat you with…" for a moment he fumbled for the word… "with disdain, is it?"

She suddenly realised that he did understand. A Syrian refugee in a foreign country where many people would have judged him by the colour of his skin and his occasionally awkward English. For a moment she felt ashamed.

"Sorry, Sarah," she whispered to herself.

Aloud she said. "But why me? I have no skills to offer."

"You are like Sarah. You are a caring person who believes in justice. I know this because she has told me so."

"Well, thank you, but…I couldn't, I really couldn't, I'd be absolutely useless. Apart from anything else, I wouldn't be able to talk to anyone."

"Kindness does not need many words. The actions are what matters. But it is true, a few words of greeting and concern are always useful."

Angie had a sudden memory of the book on Sarah's desk. "Were you teaching Sarah to speak Arabic?" she asked.

Mahir smiled again. "In a way, yes. She wasn't very good at it. But she learned enough phrases to comfort people, admire their children and so on."

"Oh."

"And I can help you do the same."

Angie fumbled round for words to express her doubts. "How long does the journey take?"

"Three or four days. It is quite hard. We often have to sleep in the van."

"And there are four of you?"

"Yes. We share the driving but we have found it is best for the ladies to drive when we cross borders. We are often stopped there and the lady drivers are treated better than the men. Sarah was very good. She laugh, she joke with border guards and we never have trouble."

Every instinct in her was saying "No, get rid of this young man. Forget he ever came. Retreat to your safe, undemanding existence."

But then she saw Sarah's letter lying on the floor and her mind flashed back to the teenage classroom where Sarah, fearlessly, stood up for what she saw was justice, regardless of the consequences.

"Well…" she began.

Mahir smiled. "*As-salaam alykum. Ant shakhs tayib.*"

"Sorry?"

"It's Arabic for. Peace be unto you. You are a kind person."

"Oh."

"When someone says *As-salaam alykum* to you the polite response is *Wa-Alaikum-Salaam* which means peace be also with you. There, that's your first Arabic lesson."

She was still not sure but she hesitated. "Well, perhaps I could meet Bella and Patrick."

Mahir smiled. "Of course."

A few days later the four of them met up one evening and she recognised Bella and Patrick from Sarah's funeral. They began talking and they got on well, helped by the shared bond in their sadness about Sarah.

She still had doubts about driving a van but Patrick put her mind at rest.

"It's a Luton, basically a large transit. Sarah told us you'd often driven a big camper van when you went on holiday. No different to that really."

She was still very nervous but she agreed to have a couple of basic Arabic lessons with Mahir and before long she could say "*I am here to help you*" and "*You have beautiful children*" and various other short, friendly phrases.

Then came the moment of decision.

Mahir said, "We are scheduled to do a relief run next month, Angie. Will you join us? Will you drive the van with us?"

Would she? She still didn't know, but apart from anything else, there was still one hurdle to overcome. She spoke to her manager, explained the situation and asked if she could have a few days off to make this trip. Part of her was hoping he'd say "No," so the decision would be made for her, but he was very impressed and gave his permission.

Now there was no going back but as the time for the trip approached she felt her stomach knot with fear. Once she even picked up the phone to say, "No, she couldn't do it," but then an image of Sarah came into her mind. Sarah, with that confident smile, Sarah who believed in her when no one else did. She did not make the call.

Ten days later they were on their way. Mahir, Patrick and Bella had been very supportive and Bella had taken her out to buy a rucksack and a sleeping bag and helped her assemble the minimum of personal belongings to see her through the days they would be on the road.

Mahir had explained that this trip was slightly different. Normally they would cross the channel and then head in a straight line towards Turkey, across France, Germany and

Austria into Slovenia. However, on this trip they had to divert to Lausanne in Switzerland to pick up more supplies that had been collected.

After Lausanne, they drove on through German-speaking Switzerland heading for the Simplon Pass to take them over the mountains and down into Italy.

Angie was driving as they began the climb up into the mountains. The scenery was magnificent – she could hardly believe that she – Angeela – was driving a van across Europe, over the Alps and on to Turkey. Her initial fear had almost vanished. She was enjoying the company of the other three and she suddenly realised she was both happy and at ease. It was a wonderful feeling. Liberating.

They reached the top of the pass and stopped for a few moments to admire the view. Then they pressed on down the steep, winding road towards the valley below.

Then suddenly, as she drove, she heard Sarah's voice as clearly as if she'd been sitting beside her.

"There you go, Angie. What did I tell you? You can do anything so long as you believe you can."

She grinned to herself, then turned to Mahir.

"Can you just have a quick look back behind us, please?"

"Yes, of course, but why?"

"I just want to make sure that the elephants are following us closely."

Then she burst into peals of laughter at the look on his face.

Just One of Those Days

I have never been terribly keen on chemical drain cleaners. In my experience, most domestic drainage problems can be solved with a good firm action with a plunger. Best not to wear a good dress while doing it, though, in case of blow back.

It was the kitchen sink this morning. Probably the grease from the Confit de Canard that we served last night. Time and time again I've told Owen to take the greasy pans into the yard and pour the residue down the outside drain.

"Yes, Madam," he says, "of course, Madam."

But he's not actually listening and nothing changes.

Of course, if the plunger fails, and sometimes it does, then you're forced back on more mechanical methods. But again in my experience, there is a limit to what you can do by unscrewing your ball trap and scraping out the grease with your fingernails. No, if the blockage lies near the plughole then you can do a lot worse than use one of those metal coat hangers you get from the dry cleaners. All you need is a stout pair of pliers, then you unravel the twisted bit where it's all joined together, straighten it out, put some kinks in it then stick it down the plug hole and wiggle it. That should get rid of your grease balls.

The plunger didn't work this morning. I wasn't surprised. Full house last night. That's twenty covers. Twenty duck thighs. A lot of grease.

As a last resort, when even the coat hanger fails to live up to expectations, you're forced back on the rods. It's quite straightforward. You lift the drain trap outside the kitchen window, get down on your hands and knees – definitely don't wear a dress for this job – bolt the rods together one by one and shove them up the pipe.

You get your hands dirty, but the job's done. And when you're running a small private hotel speed is of the essence. You don't have time to wait for some workman to come round in three days' time at fifty quid an hour and only half do the job when he does come.

I needed the rods this morning. Turned out it wasn't just the kitchen sink that was causing the problem. Bit of a drainage traffic jam all round with all the aromas that go with it.

I wonder sometimes what would happen if Councillor Richardson were to see me in my drain-rodding mode. The very thought of it makes me smile. The idea that the Vice-Chair of the Bexington Sands Tourism Committee should be flat on her belly shoving drain rods down a sewer pipe has probably never occurred to him.

He sees me as a model of gentility, always on hand to charm civil servants, rich businessmen or even the rare government minister who dares venture into the distant wastes of Bexington-on-Sea without getting a yellow fever jab first.

"Justine," he says to me, Councillor Richardson that is, "Justine, you could wheedle open the wallet of an Income Tax

Inspector just by lifting your eyelashes and murmuring in his ear how the Bexington Band Stand needs an instant re-fit. You are my secret weapon, Justine, my Polaris missile."

He gets a bit carried away, does Councillor Richardson, not to mention the fact that his style of talking is seriously out of date. But he means well. And I don't mind. In fact, to be honest, I wouldn't mind if he got considerably more carried away.

It's all a question of perception. He sees the Justine he wants to see but that is only one Justine. There are others. None of us are just one person, are we? We're a collection, a mixture, different things to different people.

The trick is to remember who you are in a particular set of circumstances.

Ah well...!

I got myself cleaned up after the rods episode but unfortunately, it turned out that the problem had not been completely solved. The next thing was that Mr Kurusaki in number 3 arrived in reception showing none of the smiling, oriental courtesy that we associate with the Japanese. In fact, he was quite expressive. It's amazing, isn't it? Oh, not just that he can speak English. I understand there are lots of Japanese who can speak English. They learn it off the BBC World Service, I'm told. No, what is amazing is his command of the...well, the vernacular, as you might say.

To be fair, Mr Kurusaki did have a point. I mean, when a visitor is paying good money for a twin-bedded room with colour telly, tea, coffee and en-suite facilities, the one thing they do not want is the lavatory backing up on them at an inconvenient moment.

Of course, when it comes to lavatories backing up virtually every moment is inconvenient.

Now I fully accept that blocked lavatories are a very different kettle of fish to blocked kitchen drains, but they all have to be dealt with so it was back into the overalls and out I went again with the rods. I found the new blockage under the waste trap by the annexe. Actually, it didn't take much finding once you arrived within a few feet of it.

Ah, well. Couldn't be helped. Just one of those days.

I got cleaned up again and went back into reception. Mr Kurasaki was still there, pacing up and down, most un-Japanese-like. I began the process of calming him down, I gave him a nice gin and tonic on the house by way of saying sorry, I explained about the rods and told him that it was quite safe for Mrs Kurusaki to go back into the bathroom.

I was just beginning to think that the crisis was over when young Kylie arrived to see her mother – that's Mrs Osborne, our Monday to Thursday cleaner. Now that, in itself does not present a problem, but for reasons best known to the child, she chose this day to bring her hamster with her. In its little cage. And that, as it happens, was an unfortunate piece of timing.

Of course, she didn't know that Mr Kurusaki is frightened of hamsters, well, as it turns out he's frightened of all small furries as the vets call them, so you can't blame the child. But it was still unfortunate. Mr Kurusaki took one look at the hamster and jumped up screaming. His G & T goes everywhere, all over the carpet, the reception sofa, everywhere.

The kid's terrified, drops the cage, the door springs open, Hammy zips out, the cat appears from the residents' lounge, spots its meals on wheels so to speak, and brings the whole performance to a rapid and final conclusion.

But even that's not all. Mrs Kurusaki, hearing her husband scream, comes rushing down the stairs, sees the cat and begins sneezing violently. Turns out she's allergic to cats. So there we all are, Mr Kurusaki gibbering in the corner, the kid crying, Mrs Kurusaki sneezing fit to bust, I'm trying to think how to say sorry all over again and the cat's sitting there with the hamster's tail hanging out of the corner of its mouth. Good social occasion. They left within the hour and didn't pay their bill.

And then the chip pan caught fire.

If I've told Owen about that chip pan once, I've told him a dozen times, but he simply doesn't listen. I got so cross a few weeks ago that I went out and bought three smoke alarms – yes, three of them – and put them all up in the kitchen. "There now, Owen," I said to him, "that should give you fair and sufficient warning when your oil is reaching a dangerous state so you can do something about it before barbecuing all your recipe books."

A few days later, the chip pan caught fire again and not a squeak out of the alarms. Of course, when I looked closely I found he'd only gone and taken all the batteries out. He said they kept going off when he was making toast and giving him a headache.

I bet Councillor Richardson never takes the batteries out of his smoke alarms.

Now, normally, the way I would deal with chip pan fires is with a fire blanket. We always keep one in the kitchen, so all you have to do is grab it off the wall and throw it over the fire, cutting out the flow of oxygen and thereby halting the combustion process. Simple. Even if we do get through rather a lot of them.

However, this morning my patience was not all it might be, what with the upset over the Kurusakis and Kylie's hamster…the lavatories and the drains…so I was in no mood to pull Owen's chestnuts out of the fire, so to speak.

I decided that drastic measures were called for. So, instead of using the fire blanket, I picked up the Wet Chemical Fire Extinguisher – that's the one with the cream label, of course, which says wet chemical fire extinguisher on it for the avoidance of doubt. With its F rating, the wet chemical fire extinguisher is extremely effective at tackling large chip pan fires and is ideal for industrial cooking environments.

Anyway, I took the WCFE and sprayed the chip pan with it and a large part of the rest of the kitchen while I was about it. Stopped the fire, of course, but the whole kitchen was covered in soapy foam: work surfaces, hobs, floor, shelves, pots and pans, everything.

Owen took one look and sagged onto the floor. "My kitchen," he screamed, "what am I going to do about dinner tonight?"

"What indeed?" I said, "but no doubt you'll think of something. Personally, I am going out. I am having lunch with Councillor Richardson."

"You cannot leave me like this," he yelled. And 'yelled' really is the only word for it.

"I can and I will," I said, "I want this kitchen spotless by the time I come back and…" At this point, I pushed my face right into his and hissed at him… "And I expect the batteries to be back in the smoke alarms. Gottit?" And I swept out.

My lunch with Councillor Richardson is the high spot on my social calendar. It all started about a few months ago when he suddenly announced that he wanted to go over the budget for the Christmas lights along the sea front with me. Apparently, there was a discrepancy between the estimate and the final bill and as Chair and Vice-Chair of the Tourism Committee we needed to form an opinion on whether this was a genuine problem of project creep – as the consultants have it – or if, for some of the contractors, Christmas had come a little early as it were.

For that first occasion, I dressed especially carefully. Lunch in a sea front café to discuss budget discrepancies was not quite the same as a candlelit dinner for two in a discreet little restaurant, but it was at least a step in the right direction.

We dispensed with the Christmas Lights problem before we'd even ordered – turned out to be a typing error on the invoice – and the rest of the meal was just…Bliss.

Of course, being the first occasion so to speak, we stuck to official business but we were both enjoying ourselves. You could tell. My lasagne was a bit lumpy. Owen, when not setting fire to chip pans, can do much better, but I wasn't there for the food.

Neither was Councillor Richardson apparently. As we were finishing our coffee Councillor Richardson looked across at me and said, rather shyly I thought, "This has been a most enjoyable occasion, Justine. Useful and enjoyable. I trust you have also found it so?"

"Oh, I have," I said, "indeed I have."

"In that case," he said, "I have a little proposition for you."

Well, I tell you, I felt little goose bumps run all down my spine but I managed to control the churning in my stomach and produced my warm slow smile. The one calculated to put people at ease but get them all excited at the same time if you know what I mean.

"Let's make this a regular event," he said, "let's have lunch once a month. It will give us the opportunity for informal consultation as well as being a very pleasant occasion. I am sure the council expenses will stretch that far without bursting."

Well, it wasn't quite the proposition I'd been hoping for but it was, as you might say, only our first date.

Since then we have met every month, shared lunch, discussed our work and our colleagues and gazed into each other's eyes. Well, I gazed into his anyway. And we'd chatter on about everyone and everything.

Except, now I look back, I see it was me who did the chattering. He who did the listening.

All the same, they've been happy occasions, a little oasis in the desert of burning chip pans, awkward guests and…

…those bloody drains.

An oasis, that is, until today.

I didn't see it coming. We had lunch as usual. I'd long since given up on the lasagne and moved onto the cottage pie. Dull, but more reliable. Councillor Richardson had his usual sausage and mash, smothered in red sauce. I've trained myself to ignore that.

During the meal we chatted about bits and pieces as usual. We both agreed that the problem with Mrs Tomkins in Accounts constantly dropping marmalade into her computer's keyboard was not serious enough to warrant further action. We also agreed not to make a formal complaint about the nature of the calendar hanging in the Doorman's cubby hole at the Town Hall entrance as that could be construed as an infringement of his human rights. I received the impression that Councillor Richardson may have secretly quite liked it.

We had finished our coffee and Councillor Richardson was counting out the tip very precisely, always ten per cent to the nearest penny, rounded down if it doesn't work out exactly, when out of the blue he said, "Justine, I wonder if you would consider doing me a little favour? Would you be prepared to come round to my house later today?"

Well, I mean to say. I had been longing for something like this, but when it finally came I found myself tongue-tied. He sensed my confusion, he's sensitive to people's feelings, is Councillor Richardson, and so he leaned across the table and patted my hand. "Shall we say, about five?"

I would have preferred to say about eight and I'll bring the wine but going there at all was progress. So I said five would be fine.

And then…

And then…

And then he said, "Justine, I need you…"

It was a heart-stopping moment. I felt a wave of emotion pour over me. I was so excited, I can't tell you. So excited that I almost missed the rest of his sentence.

"…to help me with a serious problem."

The second part of that sentence didn't seem to fit the first part if you know what I mean, so I said. "Sorry, could you just say that again."

And he did.

"Justine, I need you to help me with a serious problem. Mrs Richardson is coming home tomorrow – she's been staying with her sister in Bromsgrove – but the problem is that the bathroom drain is blocked. I've got water flowing back up the plughole into the bath and I don't know what to do."

I suppose I must have looked at him in amazement because he blushed a little and went on. "I know it is a lot to ask, Justine, but you have told me so much about your drain-clearing experience that I felt sure you would aid me in my time of need."

I had no idea I'd ever spoken to him about drains but, I'm afraid it has to be said when I start nattering on I don't always listen to what I'm saying. Somehow, during our cosy little lunches, I had changed his perception of me from his sophisticated Polaris Missile to an efficient drain cleaner.

And I hadn't known there was a Mrs Richardson.

Of course, I said 'Yes'. I didn't want to, but saying 'No' would have caused all sorts of embarrassment and at least, if I gave him a good rodding, our little lunches in the café can go on. Better than nothing.

Ah, well...

I'm afraid Owen got the rough edge of my tongue when I got back to the hotel which was a little unfair as he had actually made quite a good start on cleaning up the kitchen. He looked so woebegone that I had a change of heart, changed out of my lunch clothes into my overalls and set to and gave him a hand. By the time I had to stop the place was looking halfway respectable.

"You'll need to finish off here," I said, "I have another appointment."

Owen gave me half a smile and just nodded. I smiled at him – an unhappy chef is not good for a hotel – but I did make a very obvious point of checking the batteries in the smoke alarms before I left. All present and correct.

Ah, well. It's a quarter to five. Time to go. Got my plunger and my coat hanger and the drain rods are in the car. Well, at least I'll see inside Councillor Richardson's house, inside his bathroom in fact. Maybe he'll suggest a little glass of sherry when the job's done. And who knows? Our friendship continues. Perhaps next time his wife goes to Bromsgrove…

Not what I'd hoped though.

Still, that's life. It's just been one of those days…

That Was Lovely, Dear

GRACE

She was ready in good time. Punctuality had always been important to her. She had no idea what Jennifer had in mind but it was very kind of her and Duncan to arrange a treat for her birthday. She wasn't used to birthday treats. Even before Geoffrey became ill she had usually spent the day alone though Jennifer always phoned her from Melbourne.

In the early days after she and Duncan had moved to Australia, Jennifer would get the time difference wrong. For the first couple of years, Grace would be woken around 11.00 p.m. to the sound of "*Happy Birthday To You*" echoing from the other side of the world.

She never mentioned the fact that the call was a little premature and that she had been asleep. She was just grateful that Jennifer had remembered and wanted to speak to her mother on the day – or what she thought was the day. She was also thankful that Geoffrey slept in a different room. He would not have been amused to be woken for something as trivial as a birthday greeting. In fact, the late-night calls only happened a couple of times before Jennifer got her head round the time difference and switched to ringing around mid-morning on the day itself.

However, this year was different. When it had become apparent that Geoffrey's emphysema could only have one ending – and that very soon – Jennifer had flown over to be with her parents. She was very considerate. She booked an Air B&B nearby, so she could be on hand "without being a burden," as she put it.

JENNIFER:

I was shocked when I saw my father. True, it was over ten years since I had last been home but he had always been a big man, strong and in control. Now he was a shrunken caricature, pathetically glad to see me. There was a nurse with him when I arrived which surprised me until I realised that of course, my mother, in her eighties, could not possibly care for him in the way that he needed and Dad, as unrelenting as ever, had insisted on staying in his own home.

I had assumed my mother and I would go up and see him together but she held back. "No, you go, dear. That's fine. It's you he wants to see. I'll put the kettle on."

As soon as I saw him I was glad I'd come. It clearly couldn't be long and it wasn't. He died ten days later, almost as though he had been waiting for me to arrive before he let go. I spent time with him every day and I was with him, holding his hand when he gave one last smile – I'd always been his baby girl – and he went.

I cried, of course I cried, but my mother was remarkably stoical. Not knowing how long I would have to stay I had booked the Airbnb for two months so I was able to take care of all the funeral arrangements. Duncan and my daughter flew over for the funeral. My son was working in the UK at the time so the whole family was together for the funeral itself.

It was only later that I realised that my mother's 85th birthday was only a fortnight or so after the funeral so for the first time in years I could be with her on the day. I decided to seize the moment and organise a special treat for her. Eighty-five was quite an achievement, after all.

<u>GRACE</u>:

The funeral was micro-manged to the last napkin. The crematorium was only half full, a fact which worried Jennifer until Grace pointed out that many people they knew had, inevitably, already set out on that final journey. She could also have mentioned that Geoffrey had never been good at close friendships anyway but that seemed inappropriate in the circumstances.

She was pleased that Duncan had taken the trouble to come over for the funeral. She had always liked her son-in-law. She appreciated the way he gently handled Jennifer, letting her arrange this, organise that, then either going along with it or just doing what he had planned to do anyway. That, to her mind, was real love.

It was also a pleasure – though not one to be over-indulged – to see her grandchildren. Panda, now 27, had flown over with her father while Kuba, 31, paid a flying visit from his office in Manchester, stayed long enough to kiss his grandmother, bolt half a dozen sausage rolls and was gone again. She loved them both, in an abstract sort of way, and over the years had become accustomed to their rather puzzling names.

So now it was the morning of her birthday and she sat in the hall wearing comfortable shoes, her lightweight jacket – the day promised to be quite warm – with her handbag on her lap. She had no idea what Jennifer had planned but she assumed it would be lunch somewhere, perhaps a drive and then tea and cakes later in the day. In spite of all her years in Australia Jennifer was still very English at heart.

The doorbell rang and there they were, Jennifer, Duncan and Panda who was clutching a big bunch of roses.

"These are for you, Nanna," she said, "Happy birthday."

There was a brief hiatus as a vase was found, stems trimmed and the roses placed in the centre of the dining room table. Then they were ready to go.

Jennifer had hired a car while she was in the UK and they set off, Jennifer driving, Grace in the front beside her with Duncan and Panda in the back.

A tentative enquiry, "Where are we going?" was met with a big smile and "Wait and see. It's a surprise."

JENNIFER:

I saw this as a special occasion. The death of my father made me realise that once this visit was over and I was back in Australia I may never see my mother again so I wanted to do something special for her.

It had taken a lot of planning and I'd had to be very persuasive to arrange a couple of things, but now it was all in place. Duncan had been quietly amused at my childish enthusiasm and Panda had simply raised an eyebrow when I told them what I had arranged, but they were both willing to help me give my mother a day to remember.

As we drove I talked about my own birthdays as a child, friends from school, pass the parcel, musical chairs, jelly and cake.

"Remember that multi-coloured cake you used to make me?" I said.

My mother smiled. "Ordinary cake with lots of different food colourings. You used to call it your '*Rainbow*' cake."

"It was lovely. And everyone singing as I blew out the candles."

"I hope you're not planning a cake with eight-five candles on it," said my mother, "I'm not sure I've got that much puff these days."

"Don't worry. No candles were harmed in the making of this birthday treat."

GRACE:

The drive seemed to go on for a long while. "Surely there was someone nearer than this for lunch," she thought. Then she glimpsed a road sign as they came round a bend and suddenly had a very disturbing thought. Surely not.

JENNIFER:

We drove up the final hill I remembered so well, came over the crest and there below us and before us lay the sea with the town nestling into the bay. As a child I had always loved that view, a moment of magic for a child from an inland town.

I glanced sideways at my mother. She seemed very quiet and I assumed she was lost in her own memories. We drove along the seafront, past the boating lake and the crazy golf, turned left at the Grand 'otel – never grand enough to replace the missing 'H', and headed into the back streets of the old town.

Left, right, past the paper shop where I used to run down in the morning to fetch Dad's daily paper, then we were there. Seaview Cottage where the only view of the sea was from the attic window if you were prepared to brave the rickety ladder, the dust and the spiders. These days the cottage looked remarkably spick and span, obviously now privately owned and a long way from the somewhat tatty holiday let that I remembered.

I stopped outside, half turned towards the back seat and announced, "This is it. This is where we spent all those marvellous childhood holidays."

Panda looked rather doubtfully at the cottage. "In there? You stayed in there?"

"Yes, and it was wonderful. Quaint little rooms, a tiny staircase and you could walk to the sea in less than five minutes. We loved it here, didn't we, Mum?"

GRACE:

She smiled at Jennifer's enthusiasm but all she could remember was how much she had hated the place. Tiny, none too clean, cold. Trying to produce a half-decent meal in that inadequate kitchen was nigh on impossible and yet that was what she was expected to do while Geoffrey and Jennifer went swimming and built sandcastles on the beach. When she had tried to point this out Geoffrey had barely listened.

"It's cheap, old girl, that's the main thing. Don't have much to spare, do we, but you still need a holiday."

Except it wasn't a holiday, not for her. It was merely swapping her own organised kitchen for a much less efficient one.

"Different eyes, different pictures," she thought and out of the corner of her eye she saw Duncan giving her a glance.

JENNIFER:

I looked at my watch. The timetable for the day was pretty tight but we were right on schedule. I turned the car round and drove back to the seafront. The town was pretty much as I remembered it, though it did seem a bit smaller and there were a lot more cars around.

I managed to find a parking space along the esplanade and we got out. I took my mother's hand. "Come on, we're just in time. This is the next surprise."

We walked along the promenade to the bandstand, empty now but with rows of chairs in place.

"Remember this, mum?" I said.

"Oh, yes, dear. I remember this very well."

I turned to Duncan and Panda. "This is where mum first met dad."

They smiled and nodded.

"Mum had come here on a day out with friends from work. They sat here and listened to the music…"

"And Gramps was playing the trumpet, right?" Panda had obviously heard this story before.

"Yes, and when they'd finished he came down from the stand, walked across to your grandmother, then stood there and played his trumpet just for her. And do you know what he played?"

"'*Somewhere Over The Rainbow*', that's right, isn't it Nanna?"

"Yes, dear, that's what he played."

"Romantic or what?" I wasn't going to have my daughter stealing the limelight. "And now for the second part of the surprise. Just sit down here, Mum."

I helped her into one of the chairs, waved my hand and an elderly gentleman in a smart blazer stepped forward out of the crowd. He was carrying a trumpet and he bowed to my mother before starting to play '*Somewhere Over the Rainbow*'.

GRACE:

She sat there, stunned, not knowing whether to laugh or cry. Part of her felt angry but she realised how much effort Jennifer must have gone to in order to arrange this, effort driven by love. Whatever she personally felt, the love had to be acknowledged, so she waited until the trumpeter had finished then said, "Thank you very much. That was lovely."

The man nodded and smiled and then, as Jennifer took him off to one side, Duncan caught her eye and gave her a half smile and she smiled back.

They resumed their walk and their next stop was "*The Only Plaice*," a fish restaurant near the clock tower.

They were expected, ushered in, and given a 'reserved' table by the window. They gave their order. Duncan had a beer, Jennifer and Panda had a glass of wine and she had a cup of tea. They sat there while Jennifer told Panda – yet again, judging by the way Panda rolled her eyes – how she and her parents had come to his resort every year for their summer holiday until she was ten years old. A highlight of the week was a fish and chips supper in this place.

"Of course, in those days it was more of a café rather than a restaurant. This is quite a change."

Panda's only response was, "I can't imagine you being ten years old, Ma."

"Well, I was, once," said Jennifer a little sharply, "this place is full of memories, isn't it, mother?"

Grace had a mouthful of haddock so she just nodded.

JENNIFER:

I had been rather taken aback to discover that our little fish and chip café had turned itself into a rather swish restaurant but at least it meant I could have a glass of wine. As a ten year old my tipple was a 7-Up, much enjoyed. Back then any kind of fizzy drink was a real treat.

When we came out of the restaurant I noticed for the first time how many of the buildings along the esplanade had changed. Some were new, all of them were cleaner, and the slightly shabby look I remembered seemed to have been airbrushed away. Of course, those childhood holiday memories were nearly fifty years old but just for a moment I felt a pang of nostalgia for the past.

But that's all it was – nostalgia. I knew that I wouldn't want to stay in Seaview Cottage today and I knew that Panda would never have tolerated those simple, basic holidays that lived so vividly in my memory.

Suddenly this all felt rather uncomfortable and I knew why. Most of my memories of this place had my father in the centre of them. Tossing a ball backwards and forwards with him on the beach, him buying ice creams, eating chips out of newspaper in the early evening, him holding my hand as I tottered along the top of a breakwater. Dad, who we had buried a fortnight ago.

GRACE:

She saw the hint of tears in Jennifer's eyes and knew exactly what was going through her mind. She understood the importance of her daughter's memories of this place, even though she did not share them. As she had so often done when Jennifer was a child she reached out and took her hand and found it tightly gripped. For a moment mother and daughter shared a silent memory and then Jennifer became all brusque again.

"Time for the next treat. Come along."

She was not sure that "treat" was the word she would have chosen but Jennifer was already off, striding ahead. Duncan held back and took her arm.

"Are you alright? Not too tired?"

"No, not really." Though her shoes were beginning to pinch a little.

"Jenny so wants to give you a wonderful day."

"I know, dear."

He gave her arm a little squeeze and they walked on after Jennifer.

JENNIFER:

I wasn't sure if the lighthouse would still be there after all these years but as we came round the headland we could see it, a white finger pointing skywards on the cliff top two coves away.

"Once during the holiday Dad would let me stay up late and we would come here to see the lighthouse flashing, remember, Mum?"

"Yes, dear, I remember. And you got very excited if the weather turned misty and we could hear the foghorn start up."

"These were wonderful holidays. I've never forgotten them."

My mother took my hand again and patted it. "Happy memories are worth hanging onto, Jennifer. Never let them go, they help with the less good times."

I felt the tears begin to rise up again but swallowed them down.

GRACE:

Back into the town and the next stop was the funfair. It looked pretty run down to her but Jennifer, as usual, was full of enthusiasm.

"We loved coming here," she said, "it was all so novel in those days. Long before the big theme parks. Remember that ride, Mum, where we all sat in a tub and were whirled around."

Grace nodded. "Vividly," she said.

"It's still there. Do you fancy giving it a go?"

She was horrified but Duncan came to her rescue. "Bit soon after lunch for me," he said. "Why don't Grace and I just sit here in the sun? You take Panda. Give her a twirl."

Panda gave her father a very old-fashioned look but with a barely audible sigh went off with her mother.

Grace sank thankfully onto a bench. "Thank you, dear," she said, "I think I'm too old for twirling tubs."

Duncan just smiled.

JENNIFER:

I must confess that once we were whirling around in the tubs I began to wonder if memory was better than reality. I looked at Panda and couldn't work out if she was enjoying it or humouring me. Probably the latter. Her idea of entertainment required a keyboard and a screen.

When the ride stopped we staggered back to the others.

"Well, that was fun. Dad always enjoyed that ride." I glanced at my mother. "These memories are all very well, aren't they, Mum, but I think we might pass on the candy floss, don't you?"

"Yes," Grace said firmly. "All that sweet stuff is bad for your teeth."

"That's what you always said. That's why I never had any."

"Don't be silly, dear, of course you did. Your father waited till I had gone to the Ladies and then bought you one. I always took an extra-long time so you could finish it before I came out."

I looked at her in amazement. "You knew? All this time, you knew?"

"Of course I did, dear. I'd had my say. If your father wanted to spoil you why should I make a scene?"

"Well, I don't know…"

Duncan was smiling and Panda was openly giggling and after a moment I laughed too.

GRACE:

Dear Jennifer. Always so intense but always good-natured with it. It had obviously never occurred to her that the candy floss secret was not a secret at all. Apart from anything else the odd splodge of coloured sugar down her cardigan would have given the game away.

But now Jennifer was striding away again. "Come on, time for the next treat."

She gave a sigh and plodded after her. Panda came up beside her.

"You okay, Nanna?"

"Yes, thank you, dear."

"Strange day, isn't it? If I'm honest I find it all a bit gross but Ma really wants to give you a special treat, you know."

"I know, dear."

"And she's really missing Gramps. Well, I guess you must be too."

She was silent.

They followed Jennifer, the old woman and the young woman side by side. After a while, she realised they were heading for the pier. Thinking back over the day so far she realised that this had always been inevitable.

JENNIFER:

We walked out along the pier, over the sea and I remember as a child being slightly scared when I looked down and saw the water through the cracks in the boards. Right at the end was a tiny auditorium where, as a child, we had come to see magicians and clowns. There were sing-songs with a piano and people who told jokes I could never understand. Those evenings, once only every holiday, were another of the childhood treats that I had never forgotten.

The place was closed but I had made arrangements in advance so I tapped at the door. A young woman opened it, I gave my name, and she smiled and ushered us in.

The tiny stage had gone but the piano was still there. In the middle of the hall was a table laid for tea with balloons tied to the back of each chair. This had taken many phone calls and a lot of persuasion to arrange but it all looked lovely.

My mother looked stunned as I sat her down at the head of the table.

"Remember our evenings here, Mum? Magicians and everything?"

"Yes, dear. You must have been a magician to organise all this."

"It's your birthday tea, Mum, and there is a cake but only one candle."

Another young woman came in and sat down at the piano. She began to play "*Happy Birthday To You…*" as the cake was put down on the table.

"I thought just tea and cake, Mum, as we did have a good lunch. Now blow out the candle."

The pianist began a gentle melody of old tunes and I pretended not to see Panda sigh.

I looked at my mother, eight-five years old, and was filled with an overwhelming love for her. All those years caring for me and Dad and then just Dad. Such commitment, especially when he became ill. She deserved this treat.

GRACE:

She knew she was near to tears. Not nostalgia for this place but for the love and effort that Jennifer must have put into organising this day.

She rallied, blew out her candle and picked up her cup of tea. She was very tired but she would see this through to the end with a smile on her face.

The music was gentle, and the cake delicious. When it was all over she insisted on shaking hands with all the young women and especially the pianist.

"That was lovely, dear. Took me right back. You do play well."

The young woman coloured and smiled.

She asked to go the ladies, sat on the pan, eased her shoes off and massaged her feet. She hadn't done so much walking for a long while.

After a while, there was a tap at the door and Panda said, "You there, Nanna? Ma sent me to see if you're all right."

She opened the cubicle door. "I'm fine, dear, but you might just help me get my shoes on again."

Panda grinned and knelt down.

On the way home in the car Grace sat in the back with Duncan and Panda sat beside her mother.

As she sat there half dozing she felt Duncan gently take her hand. She turned to him and he mouthed silently, "Thank you."

JENNIFER:

The day had gone pretty well, I thought. At one stage, looking at the complex plan I had drawn up, I'd wondered if I'd bitten off more than I could chew but in the end it was all fine and my mother had seemed to enjoy it. True, she had been a bit quiet but then she always had been and it was only a couple of weeks since Dad had died.

It had been strange, re-visiting the reality of those family holiday memories. I'd put a brave face on it but it had been rather disappointing in some ways. The place had changed. Why do so many things have to change?

Still, my mother hadn't seemed to notice and the whole point of the day was to remind her of the happy times she and Dad had spent there and all the fun we'd had as a family.

GRACE:

She had been worried that they would want to come in when they got home when all she wanted to do was to take her shoes off and go to bed.

Fortunately, Jennifer seemed to understand that. She walked her up to the front door and waited while she found her key. She opened the door, then turned and gave Jennifer a big hug.

"Thank you for a lovely day, dear."

"Oh, Mum, I'm so glad you enjoyed it. What with Dad and everything I wanted to give you a day of happy memories."

"I know you did," she said, "I think you're wonderful."

There was a tear in the corner of Jennifer's eye as she went back to the car, turned and blew her a kiss before they drove away.

Grace made herself a cup of tea and took it up to bed. She was physically tired but also emotionally drained. That seaside town and the places they had visited meant nothing to her. She was not sure they ever had. But what did mean something was the love and thought and effort that Jennifer had put into arranging everything. That was priceless.

She was glad that Jennifer had been with her father when he died. They had always been close. He had given their daughter love and company and attention, all the things he had never given Grace.

That could never be explained to Jennifer. Geoffrey's long silences, his indifference to things that mattered to her, his expectations, not always stated but if not forthcoming the sulkiness that followed.

She cried herself to sleep that night, not sure if she was crying for joy for having such a loving and caring daughter or crying for sadness that she could never tell her daughter about the reality of her father.

Parking Mad

It is a truth universally acknowledged that when a group of strangers live on the same premises in close proximity to each other then disputes will arise, probably sooner rather than later.

If Patricia Gingold had ever been aware of the truth behind this travesty of Jane Austen, she would probably have thought it referred to people like students sharing accommodation. She may not have thought it applied to people who bought individual apartments in an old converted house. They were surely living independently in their own home.

The trouble was that the apartments may have been individual but the fact that the building had once been a single house meant that there were areas of common ground – garden, car park, rubbish collection area and so on. Such shared areas are always dependent on good will.

When Patricia Gingold chose to take early retirement from her post as Head Teacher of a large mixed comprehensive school in the Midlands she realised she wanted a complete change of scenery. She had a long list of things she had always wanted to do and decided that rather than go on saying "Well, I'll do that one day…" she would get on and do at least some of them now.

She also decided that the charm of the Midlands had run its course so she moved south into Sussex and Hampshire to begin looking for somewhere to spend the rest of her life. And she found it – or so she thought – in Newbolt Manor.

The house stood in apparent isolation surrounded by rolling farmland. In practice behind the line of trees to the south was an A road and a small village but neither were visible, though the roar of traffic could sometimes be heard when the wind blew from that direction.

Newbolt Manor had once been a large Edwardian house dating from the early part of the twentieth century, but it had never been a grand building. More likely it had been built to provide a home for a farm manager who would have looked after the land for an absent owner.

During the war it had been requisitioned by the army but for what purpose was never clear. The army did, however, add a couple of wings to the building, turning it from a rectangular shape into an E without the middle arm.

After the war, it was sold, becoming in rapid succession, a private school, an activity centre for young people, and a gallery for local artists (never financially viable), before eventually becoming a care home. The latter survived until the early 1990s when it fell foul of the Social Services Inspectorate, due partly to the quality of care (or lack of it) and some very imaginative accounting procedures.

After that the house stood empty until an enterprising developer bought it and obtained permission to turn it into a number of individual apartments. That was about eight years before Patricia Gingold came along.

When Patricia first saw Newbolt Manor she thought it was ideal. She liked the house, she liked the location and the apartment that was up for sale was exactly what she wanted. This was an ideal place for her retirement. What she hadn't expected was to get caught up in the kind of bullying situation that she thought she had left behind in the school.

At first, everything seemed fine. The apartment was light, bright, comfortable and spacious enough to hold all her books – or at least all those she had decided to keep. Each apartment came with two allocated parking spaces and there was additional parking for visitors. The views over the countryside were delightful and the coast was only a fairly short drive away.

But then an unexpected problem occurred.

Patricia owned a small saloon car which she used for general running around and short journeys. However, soon after moving into Newbolt Manor she also realised a long-held dream and purchased a small camper van. She had always loved regional theatre and music festivals and reasoned that if she was going to travel around to such venues it would be cheaper to find a camp site somewhere nearby rather than always be paying out for a hotel. She also had a sneaking desire, after years in a prim and proper job, to let her hair down a little.

Initially, Patricia had only used one of her parking spaces and hadn't even worked out where her second one was but once she'd bought the camper van, which she christened Hercules, she checked the plans to see where her second place was so she could park it there. Not surprisingly she discovered it was next to her existing space but the first time she came to use it she found another car parked in that spot. On that occasion she used one of the visitor's spaces and made a note to investigate further at a later date. However, the next time she came home in Hercules her second space was empty so she parked there.

Around nine o'clock that night there was a furious banging on her door and when she opened it she was confronted by Ray Hatter, another apartment owner.

"You've left your car in my space," he yelled.

"No, I haven't," said Patricia, "Both my cars are parked in the spaces I own."

"But we've always parked in the space nearest the building," said Ray.

"So what," said Patricia, "those two spaces are mine and I intend to use them."

"But we have a right to that space," said Ray, "my wife is an invalid and she can't walk from the far side of the car park."

As Patricia knew full well that both Ray and his wife Joan played tennis each Saturday morning this claim was so ridiculous that she laughed out loud. This only made Ray angrier.

"Come and move your car now," he said.

"Oh, go away, you silly little man," said Patricia and shut the door in his face.

The following morning there were two deep gashes in one of Hercules' doors, obviously done by a key. The conclusion was obvious but there was no proof. However, later that day Patricia was talking to Malcolm, who lived in the apartment above her, and she told him what had happened.

"I'm not surprised," said Malcolm, "a lot of us have fallen foul of Ray. We call him the parking Hitler as he's always finding something to complain about."

"Doesn't anyone ever challenge him?"

"Difficult. As you know there's a management committee for these apartments and he is one of the directors."

"Who are the others?"

"Well, there's James Robson. We call him King James because he's always throwing his weight about. He's in cahoots with Ray but treats the rest of us like he owns the whole building and we're his tenants." He paused. "And then there's me."

"You're a director?"

"Ye…es, but everything gets decided by the other two. They never speak to me."

Patricia thought for a moment. "What about the landlords? Can't they do anything?"

"Samuel Glossop, that's the guy from the managing agents who deals with us, is as much use as a chocolate teapot. He doesn't intervene – he simply does whatever King James tells him has been decided."

"I see," said Patricia, "well, I have to say this doesn't sound very satisfactory."

Over the next few weeks Patricia, as befitted a good head teacher, did her research and checked her facts. During this time she had to put up with a lot of minor irritations. She would come out in the morning to find the car parked next to hers was so close she could not open her door to get in and would have to scramble across from the other side. Or something oily had been put on her windscreen which could only be removed with difficulty.

No further physical damage was done to either of her vehicles but one night, returning home from a family visit in Hercules, she found Hitler Ray's car parked in her place. Her first instinct was to use one of the visitors' spaces again but then she changed her mind and parked Hercules at right angles across her two spaces blocking the other car in completely. Then she went and got her camera and photographed the scene.

The following morning about nine there was a furious banging on her door and she answered it in her dressing gown to find Hitler Ray dancing up and down.

"Your car has blocked me in," he yelled, "come and move it now."

"Oh, is that your car," said Patricia courteously. "I thought it must have been a stolen car that had been abandoned. I was just about to ring the police to report it."

"You know damn well it's my car," yelled Ray furiously.

"I know damn well it's parked illegally in my space," said Patricia.

"I demand you come and move it now."

"There's no point in shouting at me," said Patricia, "I've dealt with far worse-behaved children than you in my time."

"Are you going to move your car?"

"Yes," said Patricia, "around four this afternoon. I'll be going out then."

"But I need to go out now."

"You should have thought of that before you parked illegally." And Patricia shut the door. Five seconds later she opened it again. "Oh, and by the way, I've photographed the cars from all angles. The pictures show quite clearly that you're illegally parked and that there's currently no additional damage to my cars, so if any damage should appear…" She let the sentence hang in the wind.

In spite of her determination, Patricia was sad that such an unpleasant situation could develop so quickly over such a trivial thing but she'd never given in to bullies and she wasn't about to start now. Then a week or so later Malcolm knocked at her door one afternoon and asked if he could have a word.

"Some of the others have asked me," he began, "if you'd consider allowing your name to go forward as one of the directors of the management committee. We have an AGM at the end of the month and that would be our opportunity."

"Why me?"

"Because you're the first person to stand up to them," said Malcolm simply, "there's ten apartments in this house but Hitler Ray and King James control everything."

"But you're a director too. Can't you do something?"

"No," said Malcolm with disarming frankness. "I'm not a very strong person you see. But you could sort them, I know you could." He smiled hopefully. "I'd help, I really would, if you told me what to do."

Patricia thought for a moment. "Does there have to be a vacancy before someone else can be elected?"

"Oh, no," said Malcolm, "it's not as formal as that. Technically all the residents belong to the committee but that's not practical for day-to-day management stuff so we appoint a small group, which we call directors, to manage things on our behalf."

"And that group is Ray and James?"

"Yes, and me. I'm their nod towards democracy as you might say."

"So the full residents' committee appointed Ray and James."

"Well, yes, I suppose so. Except, well, they appointed themselves really. Just told us they'd do it and we all kind of went along with it. Less trouble, I suppose."

"But it hasn't turned out well?"

"Well, yes and no. They do get stuff done, gutters repaired, grass cut and so on but the price is high."

"You mean they charge you?"

"No, not as such. Not in money but certainly in favours. I could tell you stories of dustbin lids, door scrapers and window cleaning that would make your hair curl."

"My hair doesn't curl easily but I take your point."

There was a brief pause. Patricia was lost in thought while Malcolm looked at her with the air of a child who's been promised a treat if they behaved.

"Suppose I said 'yes'," said Patricia finally, "how many votes do you think I'd get?"

"Oh, all of them," said Malcolm eagerly, "Apart from Hitler Ray and his missus and King James of course. So will you do it? Will you stand?"

"I'll think about it," said Patricia, "and let you know."

A few days later Patricia was in the village shop down on the main road when she was approached by a lady pushing a shopping trolley.

"Excuse me. Are you the lady from Newbolt Manor?"

"I am a lady from Newbolt Manor, yes," said Patricia.

"Right. Well, my name's Daphne Rollerstone. I live in one of those houses behind the newsagents."

"Nice to meet you, Daphne."

"Yes, well, my aunt has one of them apartments up there and she tells me you're standing up to those bullies."

"Your aunt?"

"Yes, Doris Finbow, the lady in the wheelchair. A few people there have made her life a misery."

"In what way?"

"Some of them are really horrible to her," said Daphne. "That Robson man is always complaining about the ramps for her wheelchair and the handrails round the door which he says are unsightly."

"Does he?" said Patricia.

"Yes, and another man, Hamper, Hatter, Horlicks, something like that, keeps referring to her as a benefits scrounger."

"I see. That's not very nice, is it?"

"No, it isn't. So is it right? Are you going to do something about it?"

"Well, it looks like I might have to, doesn't it?"

That conversation finally made up Patricia's mind. She knew that if she said "no" to Malcolm's proposal then the petty bullying would continue and she'd have joined the ranks of the spineless ones. On the other hand, she was certain Hitler Ray and King James would not abdicate without a struggle.

And she was right. The day after her decision to stand as a director had been made public she came out of her apartment one morning to find she had two flat tyres.

She nodded thoughtfully, rang the garage and then made a few other calls. The next day was Friday and she took Hercules and headed off, coming back later that evening with two grandsons on board.

"Jack and Ben are coming to stay with me for the weekend," she told Malcolm, "isn't that nice?"

On Saturday Patricia took her grandsons shopping. On Sunday when most of the other residents were out, the three of them worked busily. On Sunday evening Hercules had another outing as she took the boys home. When she got back that evening her parking space was empty but her headlights picked up an unnatural glint and when she got out to investigate she found a big pile of broken bottles all over her parking space.

With a sigh, she went indoors, got a broom and dustpan and swept it all up before finally parking Hercules and going to bed.

A fortnight later came the AGM. During that fortnight there had been a number of other incidents. Red paint had been sprayed all over Patricia's front door. Another nail had been hammered into one of her tyres and more scratches and dents had appeared on both cars. The plants in the tubs under her windows had been ripped up and the earth scattered everywhere.

Malcolm was very upset. "I'm so sorry," he said, looking at Patricia's paint-covered front door. "I never thought they'd go this far."

"It's not a problem," said Patricia, "trust me."

The routine business of the AGM was dealt with very quickly. All the residents were present and so was Samuel Glossop from the managing agents. Glossop was chairing the meeting and he finally came to the last item on the agenda.

"Item 8," he announced, "the proposal to elect new directors."

"Directors?" said Malcolm, "I thought Patricia Gingold was the only nomination."

"There's been a last-minute candidate," said Glossop, "Mrs Joan Hatter's name has also been proposed."

"Who by?"

"By me," said Ray Hatter smugly, "and seconded by our friend, James."

Malcolm looked outraged but Patricia merely smiled. At that moment she happened to catch James's eye and detected a hint of uncertainty so she moved her smile up a gear to the one she'd used on first years who were talking in assembly.

"We'll take the names in alphabetical order," said Glossop, "So first we have a proposal to elect Patricia Gingold as a director. The proposer is Malcolm Gorland and the seconder Mrs Doris Finbow. All those in favour please raise your hands."

All the hands went up apart from Ray and Joan Hatter and James. Patricia looked straight at him, smiled again and rather hesitantly James's hand also went up.

"And against?"

Two Hatter hands were raised. "A resounding majority," said Glossop, "now the next name is Joan Hatter. The proposer is Ray Hatter and the seconder James Robson. All those in favour…"

"Just a moment, Mr Chairman." Patricia's voice cut through Glossop as though she were dealing with a noisy classroom.

"What?" said Glossop, "what's going on? You're not challenging the right of Mrs Hatter to stand, are you?"

"I'm not challenging the right for another resident to stand, no," said Patricia, "but I am challenging Mrs Hatter's right. In my view, she's not a fit person to hold public office – or any other office for that matter."

"How dare you," Hitler Ray came bounding out of his seat. "You have no right to say such things and…"

"And furthermore," Patricia went on, ignoring Ray completely, "I would like to propose that this meeting insists on the immediate resignation of Mr Hatter as also being an unfit person to hold…"

The room erupted. Hitler Ray and Joan were screaming at Patricia, Glossop and King James were on their feet, Doris was cheering and Malcolm looked stunned.

Patricia just sat quietly until Glossop eventually managed to calm things down. Then he turned to her.

"It would seem you've made two defamatory statements," he said, "Are you willing to apologise?"

"Of course not," said Patricia firmly, "my statements would only be defamatory if they were untrue."

"They are untrue," yelled Hitler Ray, "I'll sue you to hell and back, lady."

"Oh, good," said Patricia, "that'll be fun. Especially when I show these video clips to the court." She reached into her bag and produced a tablet computer. "Shall I play them now and then we can all see what we're talking about."

"What video clips?" asked Glossop.

"The ones made on the digital surveillance system my grandsons installed for me," said Patricia. "The camera covering my front door clearly shows Mrs Hatter using an aerosol to spray red paint all over it. The ones in the car park show Mr and Mrs Hatter attacking my car with a screwdriver and puncturing one of my tyres. I don't have shots of them digging up my plants but I think I've got enough, don't you?"

There was a long pause. Glossop turned to face the Hatters. "Do you have any comment to make?" he asked.

Silence. The Hatters were looking at the floor, King James sat tense and watchful. Glossop turned back to Patricia.

"This does rather change things," he said. "How do you want to proceed?"

"Well," said Patricia, "my first option is to bring charges against the Hatters for criminal damage."

Both the Hatters went white. "But," Patricia continued, "as a head teacher I do understand about petty spite and childish tantrums so I'll settle for the resignation of Ray Hatter as a director and the withdrawal of Joan Hatters' nomination."

Glossop looked across at the Hatters. "What do you say to that?" he asked.

There was a very brief pause then…

"I resign," said Ray.

"And I withdraw," said Joan.

"Thank you," said Patricia, "and once we have that in writing I'll tell my grandsons not to publish the video clips on Instagram. Although they will be very disappointed," she added.

After the meeting King James approached Patricia. "You think you've won, don't you?" he said.

"I know I've won," she said brusquely.

"But you didn't ask for my resignation and I'm still here and still a director."

"But you won't be behaving badly any more, will you?"

King James grinned. "Lady, I've not even started on you yet."

"Then I suggest you never do or the video I have showing you also attacking my car, upending the rubbish bins into my parking space and ripping up all my plants will go straight to the police."

King James went white. "You never mentioned that in the meeting."

"No, I didn't," said Patricia, "it's always as well to keep something in reserve, don't you think? Now run away and play. I've got things to do."

And so the Battle of Newbolt Manor was won. Within weeks both the Hatters and King James put their apartments on the market. The day they finally moved out the other residents invited Patricia to a small tea party.

"It was a good day for us when you moved in here," said Malcolm. "We really needed someone like you with your strength of character."

Patricia grinned rather ruefully. "Not just strength of character," she said, "but strength of nerve as well."

"What do you mean?" asked Doris Finbow.

"Well," said Patricia, "I've faced many tricky situations before but I have seldom had to bluff as I bluffed that afternoon. You see, just before the meeting, I went to check the video clips that Jack and Ben had made but discovered that I'd somehow managed to delete them completely. If the Hatters had demanded to see them I'd have been stuffed."

She looked round at a group of amazed faces.

"But they didn't, because they knew they were guilty. So I won." She grinned. "Any chance of another piece of that lemon drizzle cake, Doris?"

Snapshots

They are all there, in my mind. Not the black and white snaps, curling at the edges, falling out of their stick-on corners, creased with age like the ones in the old albums I found in my mother's sideboard. Neither are they the colour pictures, lovingly mounted with captions, that record the trips my wife and I have taken together over the years. These snapshots are just there, pictures in my mind, isolated incidents from my life, but as clear to me now as when they happened. Or when I thought they happened because I fully accept the unreliability of memory.

No matter. They are real to me and therefore they are real. And they are there. Now. When I need them. Now, when my life in the present has moved from firm ground to shifting sand. Now, when pictures from the past are so much more comforting than pictures in the present. I do not know why it's these little things – because most of them are little – have stuck in my memory, but they have. Perhaps they are not snapshots, perhaps a kaleidoscope would be a better description and yet that suggests I'm seeing them altogether like a photo montage. That is not the case. They're individual memories and I have no idea what triggers them. All I know is that they help me when I cannot sleep – which is quite often these days.

"Let your mind go blank," says the well-meaning lady who is trying to give me the basic tools of meditation. "Then picture something that is very still, very beautiful and which means something to you."

So far, almost so good. I can begin that process, but I cannot hold a single picture. In spite of all my good intentions my mind moves on, the pressures come flooding back and I am still wide awake.

I do not believe in rigidity. Change is the only constant and once we come to terms with the fact that nothing stays the same then life becomes slightly easier. So I thought to myself. "I can see what she wants me to do and I can see why. I just don't seem to be able to do it, at least not in her way. Fair enough, so let's try my way."

So I lie there in the dark, my wife breathing evenly beside me, and try and empty my mind. But then, at that simple moment of calm, instead of fixing my thoughts on one single picture I go back in time to a place or a moment in my life and focus on that. I do not make a conscious choice, I think of something – the sea, an old friend, a particular drink, a smell drifting on the wind – let my mind go blank and see what comes. A picture emerges – the centre of the album if you like – and I begin looking at the snapshots round it.

It's at this point, and I do not pretend this will work for everyone, that the detail becomes important. It is no use thinking back to a childhood holiday, that is too vague. I need to remember the walk from the boarding house to the beach, the place where the kerb is higher than the rest of the pavement, the feel of the grass as we cross the ornamental gardens, that first smell of salt and seaweed, the gritty feel of sand on my feet, the scratchy itch as I pull my socks on over the half-dried sand. So my solitary picture has become a movie but out of that movie I take stills, so in a sense I am doing what my meditation teacher has asked of me but I am doing it my way.

I am creating my own snapshots. But why one particular setting comes into my mind at one particular time I still do not know. Probably it's best I don't.

Snapshot 1950. A small boy on his way home from school with his mother, she is probably pushing my sister in a pram but that is outside this memory. The snapshot is of a newly tarred road, black and glistening and irresistible.

"Don't touch that," says my mother but of course I do. Suddenly the attractive glistening black becomes nasty and sticky and smelly.

"What did I tell you?" says my mother crossly and we go home in silence to a harsh scrubbing session with every kind of 1950s detergent available which left me in tears with red, rubbed-raw fingers.

Snapshot 1962. The old golf course long since abandoned by the formal game, is now more a kind of park, grass, hummocks, old bunkers, and a stream running along the edge. A boy, almost a young man, mid-teens, lies on the grass in the sunshine of a summer Saturday. Not unhappy but with a sense of adolescent uncertainty. I don't want to go home, I don't want to go for a long cycle ride, though my pride and joy, a drop-handlebar, lightweight bike with its 5 Derailleur gears lies on the grass beside me. What I really want to do is to see

Mary Robertson but I don't know how. We go to the same youth club but so far all I have managed is "Hello." I know where she lives but I have cycled past her house twice today already and there doesn't seem much point in doing so again. Instead, I lie in the sun, chewing a piece of grass and dreaming of walking with Mary, holding her hand and talking and talking to her. The innocence of a 1960s teenager. Or my innocence anyway.

Snapshot 1970. Older now and jealous of an old school friend who has just bought a sports car, a Frog-Eyed Sprite. All I had was a Morris Minor and I looked at his car and…but, no, I don't want snapshots of cars. Think of something else, quickly…

Snapshot 1957. A few days before Christmas. I'm eleven years old and in Hamleys Toy Shop in Regent Street. A world of magic and undreamed of delights. Being there is sufficient in itself but I am there with my friend Nigel and we have been allowed to come up to London on our own for the first time. Bus to the station, tube train to Oxford Circus. And here we are. An adventure. There is a huge working model railway, Meccano models way beyond anything I have ever built, everything from teddy bears to chemistry sets. A wonderland. I'd like to think that Nigel and I appreciated the trust that our mothers had shown in letting us come up to London on our own but I suspect such a thought never crossed my 11-year-old mind.

These are strange little windows on another world – these snapshots. Oh, I am not inventing them but I am almost certainly colouring them and why are these the ones that come to me in these dark, sleepless hours? Of course, I'm deliberately seeking happy moments or intensely vivid moments, anything to show that life is a mixture, of good times, and bad times and all you have to do is find the balance between them.

All you have to do…

It is easier to push the black thoughts away in the day, things to do, people around you, life can go on. But when the night comes and you lie there in the dark, it's then that your mind takes you to places you don't want to go. That's when I need the snapshots.

Snapshot 1964. Dartmoor, wild and bleak stretching out ahead of me. The smell of ponies and heather with a hint of petrol fumes. My first visit to the West Country. I have left school and this is my last family holiday. A strange new world opens out in front of me, the years ahead as unknown and unexplored as this vast expanse of moorland. No, of course I don't believe that was a formulated thought at the time. That is definitely a later interpretation imposed on the memory, but the vision of that landscape has stayed with me, as clear in my mind as the day I first saw it.

Snapshot 1981. Sitting with my wife on the terrace of a French café, a demi in front of us, the sun warm on our faces. The unfamiliar architecture, the conversations – only half understood – floating around us. The smell of cooking drifting out of the building. It could be any café in any town but it is definitely France, our first foreign holiday together. Life is exciting. The moment is peaceful – the first of many such moments over the years.

Snapshot 1956. Bonfire Night. The excitement which has been brooding all day bursts into flames – literally. The neighbours and their children are in our garden, boxes of fireworks everywhere. I have my own torch and so feel a sense of power in the darkness. The rockets explode, the bangers bang, the Catherine wheels spin and the guy, which we have all helped to build, starts to burn, complete with the inexplicable label my dad has hung round its neck which just says "*Nasser.*" Happiness. Security.

These – and others like them – are the night-time snapshots, the little calm oases which give me comfort and, on a good night, eventual sleep. They are random, they are my past – or a version of it – but I know deep down that all they really are is escape.

"Give it time," say well-meaning friends. Perhaps they're right, but it's been six months now and, for me at least, there doesn't seem to have been much healing. And there will never be any healing for her, will there?

I've tried the pills – a waste of time. I've had the counselling – well-meaning but ultimately empty. Now I'm giving meditation a go. Adapting it to my own style. It is giving me more sleep but it's not solving anything. Not surprising really. The only solution is acceptance and that is still beyond me.

I am learning there are snapshots I cannot avoid but I know I can't take them neat. I have to face them, turn them over again in my mind but they need to be diluted or I would scream out loud. And yet these unwanted snapshots, the way I see them, are they any more accurate that the ones from childhood? Will they too become sanitised as time passes?

Snapshot 2011. Driving through the lanes in the sunshine. Going to our local town, visit to the bank, buy a new pair of shoes. Not a care in the world.

A recent snapshot but already a false note. Of course, I had a care in the world. There are always cares. The electricity bill, a letter not written, a meeting to prepare for, ironing to do, illness of a friend. Always cares of some kind – different levels, different intensities. But you can't hold everything in mind at once so we select, prioritise, and make lists if you're like me. So, yes, I had cares that morning, must have done, but I wasn't thinking about them. I was enjoying the drive and the sunshine.

Snapshot 2011. Edge of town. Traffic lights. Green. Not far to go now. Short stretch of road with car dealers, wood yards, and light engineering firms on either side. Road I know well.

And this is the moment I dread. Was I paying attention? Was I thinking ahead to the shoes I was going to buy? Was I on auto pilot? I've been driving for over 45 years so I'm experienced. Am I too experienced? A thousand questions and no answers.

Snapshot 2011. The road ahead…

No, I can't face the next picture. Not immediately. Find another. Quickly.

Snapshot 2006. The day we moved into the cottage. Boxes all round us. Chaos everywhere but surrounded by fields. A woodpecker at the end of the garden. A stream across the meadow. A new life. A new beginning for both of us.

After all those years in the home counties, commuting, working long hours, we finally broke free. A gamble perhaps, moving so far, and into a tiny rural village in an area unknown to us, but in a very short space of time we knew the gamble had worked.

Snapshot 2011. The road ahead. A builder's van ten yards in front of me.

Why do I remember it was a builder's van? Traffic is not moving fast but I'm not too close. Would it have been better if I had been closer? But I always try and keep well back.

Snapshot 1963. Lessons in the driving school's 105E Ford Anglia. 997 cc engine, 4-speed gear box. "Always be aware of the traffic around you," says my driving instructor as we drive down Wimbledon High Street. "You can't control the space behind you, but you can control the space in front."

Since then I have driven many different cars in many different places, all over the world, Europe, America, and New Zealand. Always remembered his words 'control the space in front'.

Control. We like to think we're in control but are we? Really? It's amazing how fast your life can change. One moment happy, relaxed, engaged in a task I have done a hundred times before. Next…

Snapshot 2011. She's there. Right in front of me. Where has she come from? Inches in front. Less than inches. Nothing I can do. Crunch.

Instinctively I hit the brakes but it's too late. It was always too late. Piecing it all together afterwards, police reports, witness statements, it seems she stepped out straight in front of me. Nothing I could have done. Eventually established no blame attached to me – but that's later. At the time all I knew was that I had hit an old lady and she was lying very still in the road while another, younger woman – daughter as I later discovered – screamed abuse at me. She's in shock of course. But then, so am I.

Snapshots 2011. My head whirls through a series of pictures. Stop frame animation more than snapshots.

- The police arrive.
- I am out of the car and leaning against it.
- A policeman is on his knees beside the older woman.
- The younger woman is also on her knees and sobbing.
- The old lady is very still.
- Traffic jammed up everywhere – other drivers, and passers-by all crowding round.
- Ambulance arrives – old lady taken away.
- Policeman cautions me – just like on the telly – and asks me what happened.
- Everyone around is chipping in.
- They breathalyse me and do a drug swipe. Drugs? Me?

- Policeman's radio crackles. From his expression, I know it is not good news.
- I am formally arrested on suspicion of causing death by dangerous driving.

It is a curious experience and all the time I feel it must be happening to someone else. I'm taken to the police station where they interview me under caution. They tell me that the old lady was not badly injured physically but she had died in the ambulance, presumably from shock. The policeman is very kind. He makes no judgement. As a matter of routine they check my licence, my insurance, my speed, my health. All are fine.

I am released on bail and taken home. The police keep my car for a few days to check it is roadworthy.

A few other drivers who stopped and several passers-by all confirm that the old lady had not looked, simply stepped off the kerb right in front of me. Her death is not my fault. There is nothing I could have done.

The accident investigation confirms all the statements taken at the scene. All potential charges are dropped.

Snapshot 2011. The funeral. The coffin in the chapel. The coffin that I caused.

I am advised not to go to the funeral but I have to. I stay at the back, trying to keep out of sight, but the daughter spots me. After the service, she comes over and I brace myself for more aggression but it doesn't come.

Instead, she apologises for her outburst at the time. Her mother had become a bit absent-minded and friends have told her it was not the first time she had stepped off the kerb without looking. Previously she had been lucky. This time she wasn't. Nor was I.

"Please don't blame yourself," the daughter says. But who else do I blame?

The snapshots of my life that I cling to in the night have been lovingly polished and selected. There must have been bits in between that were not so cosy, not so comforting, but if that is so they have gone, not remembered, deleted from my hard disk of memory.

Perhaps in time I can delete the 2011 snapshots too.

I do hope so, but deep down I don't think I can. The daughter may have forgiven me but I cannot forgive myself.

There's A Slight Depression Centred Over Britain

The First Book of Rawlings

1. In the beginning was a plank and the plank was without form. Well, not entirely without form, of course. Naturally, someone had trimmed it and flattened it and given it a reasonably smooth edge, otherwise it would still be a chunk of tree and not a plank at all.

2. But the plank was without form and darkness was upon the face of the plank. And Mr Rawlings said...

"Dark as Hades in here. Let's have some light."

3. ...and he opened the shed door. And there was light. And the light shone upon the plank and Mr Rawlings said...

"That's a nice plank. I just need a few more like that and then I can start work on my ship."

4. That's me, though I'm not a ship, I'm an Ark, yes, that's right, an Ark. However, although I am inanimate, and as yet incomplete, without me there is no story so you can either accept me as your storyteller or stop now and go and read something else.

"Now, where did I put that hammer?"

5. And thus it was – thanks to the genius of Mr Rawlings – I was born, for Mr Rawlings looked upon the plank and saw that it was good. But the world did not see it was good and Mr Rawlings was mocked for his beliefs.

"'*Nutty Noah of Norfolk*'. I despair of journalists."
"We're not all like that, Mr Rawlings."
"Hmm. I'm sorry, what did you say your name was?"
"Malcolm Dreesman, Mr Rawlings. I'm from the local radio station – Meadow Sound. I've come to interview you about your Ark."
"It's not an Ark, it's a ship. How many times do I have to say that?"
"Hang on, I'll just get the recorder running. Ahem. One, two, three, testing. Right then, Mr Rawlings, I understand you're a retired engineer who thinks it is going to rain forever. Is that right?"
"I didn't retire – I was sacked. And I'm not an engineer. I'm a marine biologist with an interest in climatology. And I don't think it's going to rain forever. But I do know that it will start raining eleven months, two weeks and four days from now and it will continue without a break for at least a further nine months, three weeks, one day and four hours. That's an approximate estimate, of course."
"That's a long way ahead even for a long-range forecast."
"This isn't a forecast. It's a fact."

"Which no one else agrees with."

"Not with the timescale, no. Government bodies agree that sea levels are likely to rise but they're talking about the critical moment being the end of the century. I say we have a little under a year. It's not just the unprecedented level of continuous rainfall, it's also the question of the ice caps."

"What about them?"

"We've known for some time that they're melting faster than usual but by my calculation, the melting will accelerate rapidly once the continuous rain starts…"

"In eleven months, two weeks and four days from now."

"Precisely."

"And you believe these changes you forecast are due to the greenhouse effect?"

"The greenhouse effect, the ozone layer, global warming, the behaviour of deep-sea crustaceans, too many cars, dumping of nuclear waste, reliance on fossil fuels, short-term planning and the arrogance, corruption and stupidity of politicians. The bubble is about to burst."

"What bubble?"

"The bubble of ignorance and complacency. The attitude that says it'll never happen and even if it does, it won't happen here. Well, it's about to happen. Not just here, but everywhere."

"Oh…Um…what's going to happen precisely?"

"It's going to rain – everywhere in the world – without ceasing for at least nine months, three weeks and one day. Coupled with increased ice melt in the polar regions my calculations show that everything below the 300-metre line will be under water this time next year."

"How high are we here?"

"Around 80 to 100 hundred metres, give or take."

"So according to you, we're all doomed."

"You are, I'm not. That's why I have started to build my ship."

"Ah, yes, your Ark…"

"Ship…"

"…which you are building in your garden."

"What I do in my garden is my business."

"So long as you don't upset the neighbours or frighten the horses."

"True, but in just over eleven months, one week and two days from now there won't be any neighbours or horses, so I think the question is academic."

"Okay, so how's the construction of the Ark…?"

"For the last time, it's a…ship…"

"…coming along?"

"Um…Well, slowly I must admit. I'm having a little trouble translating the theory into reality. Wood is funny stuff, you know."

"Okay, Mr Rawlings, let's cut to the chase. What's this really all about? You can't seriously believe that we're in for another global flood? I mean the last one was yonks ago and even that's usually thought of as a myth."

"I see. Your argument is that because the earth has never been flooded before – or at least not for a very long time – therefore it cannot happen."

"Well, yes."

"Poppycock."

"Oh, I get it…it's one of those situations where you exaggerate the risk so the actual reality won't seem so bad."

"Don't be silly. I'm a scientist, not a politician."

"You're also an alarmist. Don't you think that all this talk of floods and arks…"

"For the very…last…time, it's a ship…"

"…might frighten people?"

"Clearly not, as no one believes me."

"Well, it's hardly surprising, is it? You see, Mr Rawlings, I'm trying to work out how serious you are. I mean, supposing, just for one moment, you really believe all this, you presumably plan to take…um…hang on I've got the quote here…Ah, yes…"

6. The precise words are "Every living thing of all flesh, two of every sort into the Ark to keep them alive and they shall be male and female, of fowls after their kind, of cattle after their kind, of every creeping thing of the earth after their kind."

"Not a chance, Malcolm. Well, I daresay there'll be a few spiders, there's always spiders in my experience, but frankly you're missing the point."

"So you don't want to save the world?"

"No. I don't give a stuff about mankind. I know what's going to happen. I've passed that information on to the government and been ignored. I've spelt it out for the national press and been vilified as a loony. If no one's interested, then that's fine by me. I'll take care of myself…By the way, can you swim?"

"Well, no, I can't actually."

"Probably just as well. It would only prolong the agony. Best to get it over and drown quickly when the time comes."

The Book of Arkwright

1. And lo, it came to pass that in the twenty-first century, the weather went all weird and wobbly. There was a blight upon the face of the domestic tomato crop, Manchester held the UK sunshine record, people living near rivers had serious problems with their insurance premiums and the sound of sawing was heard in the land. Oh, and that very young journalist man came back.

"Sorry to bother you again, Mr Rawlings, but the radio station has made me Ark Correspondent. Who's that out there doing all the sawing?"

"Oh, that's Ted. After your last visit, Malcolm, I realised that I could use a bit of help with some of the…um…practical work. You know. And Ted's got his own screwdriver. One of those wiggly, ratchet things. Terribly useful for a job like this."

"Mr Rawlings, don't you find it disheartening after all those years as a respected government scientist to be held up to ridicule in this way?"

"Not really. Working for the Civil Service is a bit ridiculous anyway. It may occasionally be civil but it hardly ever gives a service. No on the whole I'm quite happy to be out of it."

"Um, I think the man with the saw is trying to attract your attention."

"Yeah, I am. Now then, Mr Rawlings, can I borrow this young fella-me-lad? I need someone to hold some planks while I cut them."

"Righty ho. Oh, I don't think you've met, have you? Malcolm, this is Ted Arkwright."

"Arkwright? Is your name really Ted Arkwright?"

"Yes. So what?"

"Nothing Just seems an amazing coincidence you working on a project like this, you know."

"What's so amazing about the name 'Ted'? Come on, grab the end of that plank."

"Oh, okay. Um…Mr Rawlings, why are you really convinced this flood's going to happen? No one else thinks so."

"Probably just as well. If anyone agreed with me there'd have to be a very different strategy. I mean just think of it, in Great Britain alone you're going to have about sixty million people swimming like the clappers in less than a year from now. Well that's not a long-term plan for survival, is it?"

"Nah, but pound to a penny they can't all swim."

"That's true, Ted. Suppose that's…um…say eight per cent. That'll bring the figure down by four point eight million."

"And there'll be a few more craftsmen like me so some will have their own boats, I dare say."

"Yes, but they won't last long. Their supplies will run out."

"Ah, yes, the News Editor wanted me to ask about that. What you going to do about supplies on the Ark?"

"Ship. Well, you tell your News Editor that Mum's the word, Malcolm. Can't expect me to reveal everything to the press."

2. I know not how long it took to build my predecessor but if Mr Rawlings' prediction is to be believed then it behoves those involved in my construction to get a move on.

"Oy, can we get on with a bit of boat building please?"

"Have you built a lot of ships, Mr Arkwright?"

"Too right, I have, son. But this is my first Ark."

"But why are you so keen to help?"

"Simple. The world may mock Mr Rawlings, but it despises me. It despises everyone who has a skill, and who believes in quality and service. Cheap, tatty, break it, replace it – that's the world we live in and it sickens me."

"Right. See your point."

"So this is a chance to use my skill. I've got up a proper design and sorted out the necessary materials. Of course, we've had to make The Ark a bit bigger so there'd be room for me, my toolbox and my goldfish."

"Your what…?"

"I'm not leaving Ajax behind and if I'm helping to build this thing then I want a place on board when the waters cover the face of the earth. I'm one of the eight per cent of non-swimmers, you see. Oh, while I think of it, Mr Rawlings. I don't suppose we'll need an engine on the Ark, will we?"

"Ship. No of course not. We're not going anywhere. All we need to do is stay afloat until the waters subside. Somewhere in the region of eighteen months, I reckon, give or take a week or two."

"Going to need lots of space then so we'd best crack on. So, radio guy, are you helping or are you just going to ponce about all afternoon?"

"Well, I still think you're bonkers but it sounds like fun so, yes, sure, I'll give you a hand."

The Book of Crombie

1. Part of Mr Rawlings' prophecy has already come to pass. Winters are warmer, polar bears and gin drinkers are worrying about the shortage of ice, many people who retired to the coast have seen their only asset slip gently into the sea and the weather has become even more violent and unpredictable.

"If you come over here and look at this model Mr Rawlings, you can see I've put the main storage low in the hull, help hold her firm."

"Fine by me, Ted."

"Now how much accommodation are we going to need."

"Well, it's a bit hard to tell. I mean at the moment there's just me, my housekeeper, Mrs Postlethwaite, who insists on bringing her budgerigar. Then there's you, Ted…"

"And my goldfish."

"Fine. And your goldfish. But that's it."

"Hang on, what about me?"

"Ah, coming round to our way of thinking, are you, Malcolm?"

"It's insurance, Mr Rawlings. If you're right, I'm coming with you. If you're wrong, I get to make a prize-winning radio documentary. You can find room for me, can't you, Ted?"

"I think we'd better allow plenty of space. Best to have too much rather than too little. We're going to be in this Ark…"

"Ship…"

"…for some time, after all. Hang on, who's this?"

2. And there came unto the area wherein I was being built, a man with doubt in his heart and his collar back to front.

"Beware of false prophets, which come to you in sheep's clothing, but inwardly they are ravening wolves. Are you this Mister Rawlings?"

"Who the hell are you?"

"Unless the Lord builds the house, he who builds it labours in vain."

"I'm not building a house. I'm building a ship."

"It doesn't do to take these things too literally. The principle, as it were, should apply to any form of construction."

"Well, if you want to help that's another matter. You can give Ted a hand by nipping outside and start shifting that pile of planks over to the stocks."

"Well, I have to confess that I was speaking metaphorically…"

"No time for metaphors. There's a flood coming."

"Ah, now, there I must disagree with you. Oh, I am sure you're right about the rain. I daresay we'll have rising rivers and people sleeping in village halls while they calculate the insurance claims. But a Flood – in the sense that I understand you are forecasting – no."

"Well, that's very interesting. Meteorologist, are you?"

"No. I am a man of God. Arnold Crombie, Vicar of St Christopher's."

"I see. Well, my conclusions are based on a detailed research programme, scientific observation and many years' experience. May I ask what your conclusions are based on?"

"Rainbows."

"Rainbows?"

"Rainbows. Have you never seen a rainbow glistening in the light of the sun, Mr Rawlings?"

"Not often. If it's raining I stay indoors."

"A practical man, I perceive. Well, the rainbow was a gift from God, a promise that never again would he subject the world to a total Flood which would wipe out man and beast."

"Excuse me, sir."

"And you are?"

"Malcolm Dreesman, Meadow Sound Radio. I want to ask about the fish. They wouldn't have drowned, would they? Perhaps that's why Jesus worked with fishermen. He knew what a good job they were doing trying to use up surplus stock."

"Well, young man, I think you may be straying a little from the point?"

"No, he isn't. The point being, that you're suggesting that another flood is a theological impossibility. But the flood that's about to hit us has nothing to do with God."

"Oh come now, Mr Rawlings. Everything has something to do with God…"

"…from whom all blessings flow."

"Exactly, young man. And a few non-blessings as well. I cannot deny it."

"Leave this to me, Malcolm. God has nothing to do with it. I am talking about Man. Man who's interfered with the natural balance of nature. Man…"

"…And woman…"

"…thank you, Ted. Let's just accept that for the purpose of this peroration, I'm using 'man' as a collective noun for people. Okay."

"My dear sir, are you saying you do not see this Flood – this impossible Flood that you are predicting – as a sign of wrath from the Almighty?"

"Of course not. This is Man reaping where he has sown. If you insist on mucking about with a perfectly functional universe then something's bound to go pop. There's nothing we haven't meddled with in our arrogance and ignorance so the natural balance of things has been upset."

"This sounds like blasphemy."

"Ah, I wondered when that would crop up. The strict definition of 'blasphemy' is 'evil speaking' or 'defamation'. It's only come to be associated with God by extension."

"But even by that definition, you're blaspheming against my God – whether you accept him or not."

"I suppose I am. So what?"

"Don't you feel this is wrong? That my beliefs are entitled to some protection?"

"In the purest sense, yes. But where do you draw the line? What about my beliefs? Shouldn't they be respected too?"

"You've just said that you don't believe in God."

"But I do believe we're about to have a flood and that once it starts raining it won't stop until the waters cover the face of the earth. So, by definition, if you mock those beliefs you're also guilty of blasphemy."

"As in 'evil speaking or defamation'? Hmm. Tricky."

"Matters of conviction are always tricky."

"Mr Rawlings, can you not see that your very statement that the waters will cover the face of the earth is a direct insult to God?"

"God is an abstract term. You can't insult abstract terms."

"Now that is blasphemous."

"Why is it that this blasphemy lark only ever seems to flow one way? Why should my belief in the total flood we're about to experience be any less sacrosanct than your determination to cling on to out-dated myths?"

"My beliefs are shared by millions of others, Mr Rawlings, but as I understand it, no one, not even other scientists, support your views. In fact, you're the only one who believes that this potentially calamitous event is going to come to pass."

"So you're claiming the moral high ground purely on the basis of numerical superiority?"

"The majority is always right, Mr Rawlings, regardless of the actual truth."

"Aha!"

"No, no, I mean if I continue with my assertions that what you're building here is blasphemous, then it's only you, I am offending. Whereas if you continue to make the assertion that this non-theological flood will definitely happen, you're certainly offending Christians and probably a lot of other people as well."

"I wish to offend no one. My views have been advanced and rejected and therefore I act alone."

"Arrogance. You are right. The rest of the world is wrong."

"Conviction. I know I am right. The rest of the world only thinks it is."

"Um…hang on a tick, Vicar."

"Yes, my man?"

"Mr Rawlings isn't alone. I'm helping build this Ark because I believe him."

"But why are you so certain he's right?"

"'Cos the government thinks he's wrong. Stands to reason, don't it."

"Oh…I see…well, Mr Rawlings. I cannot agree with your conclusions but I do admire honest conviction. You are clearly sincere in what you believe, so may I just point out one little problem with your plans? Assuming that, due to some celestial oversight, your predictions turn out to be correct, then this Ark…"

"…ship…"

"…isn't large enough. You're going to be hard pushed to cram two of every living thing of all flesh; of fowls after their kind, and of cattle after their kind…"

"Why's everyone obsessed with the book of Genesis?"

"…of every creeping thing of the earth after his kind, two of every sort which shall come unto thee to keep them alive…You'll never fit all of those into that space as well as your good selves, and therefore the Ark…"

"…ship…"

"…isn't large enough."

"I was actually planning to be more selective than that. We have to be practical and in any case, this is a golden opportunity to get rid of Chihuahuas."

"If I might have a word, as the shipwright so to speak."

"Of course, my dear fellow."

"Then why not…Um, be careful with that screwdriver, Vicar…No, if you're worried about all that, why not change your mind and join us?"

"Join you?"

"Sure. We're going to need a lot of unskilled labour if this Ark…"

"…Ship…"

"...is going to be ready on time. So if you were to replace your frock..."

"...Cassock..."

"...with a pair of overalls and grab a chisel, you could not only keep an eye on the arrangements for shipping a certain amount of livestock but..."

"...Ah...I would also be reserving a place on board."

"Exactly. That okay with you, Mr Rawlings?"

"Oh, sure. Let's add another cabin, why not? Just keep an eye on his centre of gravity."

"Hmm. Well, there's certainly nothing in the scriptures that forbids me to take out insurance, so, yes, thank you, I will accept your kind offer."

3. So my size must blossom still further to serve my destiny but at least with four people helping, I will grow at a much faster rate, though in the case of the Vicar, I fear that enthusiasm far outweighs skill.

"There's just one slight problem."

"And that is?"

"What's a chisel?"

The Second Book of Rawlings

1. Darkness is appointed and it becomes night, In which all the beasts of the forest prowl about. And it came to pass that in one such period when darkness covered the face of the earth my very being was violated.

"Mr Rawlings, what's going on?"

"Someone's had a go at the Ark, Malcolm, that's what."

"What do you mean? 'Had a go at it?'"

"Someone tried to set fire to it last night."

"But why? Who'd want to do a thing like that, Mr Rawlings?"

"Frightened people, Malcolm, made even more frightened by the hysterical baying of the media."

"I don't bay Mr Rawlings. Or not about this anyway."

"I know that, Malcolm but the publicity feeds upon itself."

"Was it local people? I can't believe it."

"Probably some of them reporters making sure the story stays interesting."

"Now then, Ted, be charitable. We don't know who it was."

"Have you called the police?"

"No point. Don't forget I'm seen as a rebel. My findings were considered by the Ministry and rejected. Therefore there is no problem. Therefore the fact that I'm trying to take steps to deal with it is, by implication, a criticism of the government. I'm not saying they would themselves arrange the destruction of my…um…Ark, but don't think they'd be too upset if it happened."

"But that's terrible. What can we do?"

"I don't know. There are so few of us to build it in the time. If we have to mount a twenty-four hour guard as well then we'll never get it done."

2. And then cometh, as if in a vision, an Angel, perchance from heaven in a chariot though it appeared more like unto a motor scooter. And she spoke thus unto Mr Rawlings.

"Oh, you. You with the fancy waistcoat and the silly moustache."

"Are you talking to me, young lady?"

"Natch. I think I have an answer for you."

"And who might you be?"

"Magdalena Morris, Trainee vet."

"Oh, wow…!"

"Down, Malcolm. Well, Miss Morris, what is your interest in this matter?"

"The saving of animal life, Mr Rawlings. Is it true you're building an Ark?"

"Oh, no. Look, let's get one thing straight, Miss Morris. We have limited space. I'm not having any of this 'two by two' nonsense. I've already argued that one out with the Vicar."

"My interest is conservation, not religion. If I can guard your Ark from intruders can I join the team with a select list of breeding pairs of available fauna?"

"How can you protect my…um…Ark?"

"Geese. I'll just give them a whistle."

3. Behold the fowls of the air: for they sow not, neither do they reap, nor gather into barns, but verily they do a nice line in the protection racket.

"That's my secret weapon, Mr Rawlings. You don't argue with geese."

"Isn't she just…Wonderful."

"Down, Malcolm. Well, Miss Morris, I suppose it's worth a try."

The First Book of Passion

1. And so I was surrounded by a protective gaggle. And where the gaggle was, so was Magdalena. And where Magdalena was, so was Malcolm, for love springs eternal in the human breast, especially when you get to stand on the deck at midnight with your (undeclared) beloved by your side.

"It's rather eerie up here at night Isn't it, Magdalena?"

"D'you think so? I rather like it."

"Amazing how tall the Ark is already. I can see right over the trees towards the A140."

"Can't relax yet, Malcolm. Still an awful lot to do."

"Oh yes. I'm keeping a series of recordings you know, so we can make a full-scale documentary about all this when it's all over."

"If it ever is."

"Oh. So you really believe it's going to start raining and never stop again."

"Of course. Don't you?"

"I suppose I hadn't really thought about it properly up to now. I just sort of, well, trusted Mr Rawlings somehow."

"Quite right. He's a good egg. Doesn't waffle."

"The world's full of waffles."

"And bullshit."

"Yes, that too. Um…the moon's jolly fine, isn't it, Magdalena?"

"It is. Sad to think that soon it won't have anything to shine on. Nothing except the endless waters covering the face of the earth."

"And the Ark."

"Oh, yes. And the Ark."

"Magdalena. You will be coming with us? On the Ark I mean."

"Oh, yes. Malcolm. I'm most definitely coming. From the first moment I heard about Mr Rawlings and his Ark I knew my destiny had been revealed to me."

"That's nice. Er…what sort of destiny exactly?"

"Saving the animal kingdom – or at least some of it. Suddenly everything became clear. I only decided to become a vet because I hated office work but poking around a dog's tonsils isn't all it's cracked up to be. So when all this cropped up I saw my chance to do something useful. It may be a catastrophe, Mags, I thought, but it's also a challenge. Go for it."

"Gosh, I think that's wonderful."

"So here I am and…hang on. What's that?"

"Something's upset the geese."

"I can hear that. But what?"

"Look, Mags, there's someone over there in the trees at the edge of the road."

"Come on. After them. Tally Ho… Go get him, my beauties…"

2. It is written that one swallow doth not make a summer, but a gaggle of geese will be a match for any foe.

"What's going on?"

"An intruder, Mr Rawlings, but Magdalena's geese scared them off before they did any harm. Whoever it was she nearly had him only she tripped over a hedgehog and the intruder made his escape."

"Attracts animals like a magnet that one. Not sure it was such a good idea asking her along."

"It was a marvellous idea, Mr Rawlings. She'll be invaluable. We couldn't do without her."

"Aha. I see. Like that is it Malcolm?"

"Like what?"

"That."

"I just thought it would be useful having a vet in the crew."

"Of course, you did, Malcolm. Never mind. The geese must have given him a good fright anyway Don't suppose we'll see him again."

The Book of the Job

1. Do you see a man skilled in his work? He will stand before kings; he will not stand before obscure men. However, with only one man skilled in his work my construction did not proceed apace, more like a slow crawl.

"How you getting on, vicar?"

"Nearly finished the sharp end, Mr Rawlings Bit tricky fitting these wotsits into the pointy bit."

"I suppose not even God can require his servants to have all abounding knowledge but you'd think any member of an island race could do better than 'pointy bit', wouldn't you?"

"He's a very willing worker, Mr Rawlings. Oh, and do we have any more No. 10 screws?"

"In the tobacco tin."

"Ta."

2. It is written that the craftsman stretches out his rule, he marks one out with chalk; he fashions it with a plane. The labourer has not the skill but can only bring enthusiasm to the work.

"Oh, Mr Rawlings, can I go on board and measure up the front storage pens? I thought I ought to see about ordering enough straw."

"You can, young lady, but don't forget I want to see a list of the wildlife you're proposing to bring aboard before you begin embarking on it."

"Okey-dokey. Oh, that reminds me, Mr Rawlings. A woman called to see you while you were out. Wouldn't leave a name but said she'd call back later."

"What did she want?"

"Didn't say. She was very mysterious. Had a scarf pulled up right round her face and spoke in a deep throaty whisper. 'Tell him I'll be back', she said, 'and he'd better be here'."

"Well, that's daft. How can I be here unless I know when she's coming? Did you see her as well, Malcolm?"

"No, but perhaps it's serious Mr Rawlings. Perhaps she's from the Police. Perhaps you need a licence to build an ark in your back garden."

"Well, I have nothing to fear. When the world as we know it is about to come to an end then petty bureaucracy loses all its threat."

The Book of Unbelievers

1. And lo, as the days passed there appeared unto them a woman in black saying, "I will also set my face against that man and will cut him off from among his people because he has given some of his offspring to Moloch." Well, it was something like that. What she actually said was…

"Is your name, Rawlings?"

"Yes. Who are you?"

"Never mind who I am. Who are these people?"

"They're my crew."

"Get rid of them."

"Now just a minute, lady, are you looking for a 9 mil drill bit up your…?"

"Easy, Ted."

"I wish to speak to you alone, Rawlings."

"Well, you can go on wishing. I don't want to speak to you."

"Just leave her to me, Mr Rawlings I've got a couple of spare bags of cement and the Ark could do with a bit more ballast."

"Ballast? What's he mean, ballast?"

"Ted is suggesting that we should give you a quick coating of cement and pop you down in the hold."

"In the hold? Why?"

"Well, you see a ship requires some stability If you have a good weight low down in the hull then she will stay upright even when the sea gets rough."

"But you can't do that. I get sea sick."

"No problem, missus. By the time I've given you a cement overcoat, you won't feel a thing."

"We could just find out what she wants, Ted. before we incorporate her in the ship's structure."

"Seems a waste of time."

"Well, let's just try. You, Official Looking Person, what do you want?"

"You must stop building this Ark."

"Ship. Why?"

"Well let's just say it would be in your own best interests to stop."

"Oh no, it wouldn't. By my calculations, we only have a few months of normal weather left to us and after that, you'll need more than a pair of green wellies to keep the water out."

"Come now, Rawlings We're both intelligent people…"

"A debatable statement…"

"Don't underestimate yourself."

"I wasn't. Look, we're working to a very tight deadline here and you're delaying us with your little games."

"Games. I'm not playing games."

"Nor are we. We're talking survival here, Ms Official Looking Person."

"Why persist in this folly which can only cause you grief?"

"'Scuse me, Mr Rawlings. Look, lady, I'm the shipwright round here and if I don't get this ship finished it'll cause us even more grief to find ourselves five fathoms down and not even a plank to hang on to."

"Oh, come now. How you people can possibly believe this discredited scientist and his…his…absurd fantasy is beyond me."

"Ah, but you see, Ms Official Looking Person, Ted's point is that we do believe it. We believe it so implicitly that your threats mean nothing to us. We've set ourselves the task of completing this Ark before the rains begin so that some part of humanity will survive. It's too late to stop the catastrophe itself so damage limitation measures are the only thing left to us."

"You cannot seriously believe that it's going to start raining and never stop again. The suggestion's too fantastic for words."

"I am a scientist. I do not deal in fantasy. The only possible objection you can have to my theory is that a) no one else accepts it and b) such a thing has never happened before."

"Ahem…I don't think we can leave Noah out of this entirely."

"Thank you, Vicar. Apart from the incident involving Noah which is hardly a recent precedent. And, if I might say so, subject to some doubts about the accuracy of the reports of the event."

"Now listen to me, Rawlings. I don't think you understand. If you don't stop building this…this…outrage of your own accord, then steps will be taken to, how shall I put it, persuade you."

"Why?"

"You are spreading alarm and despondency. You are inviting insurrection."

"Rubbish. No one believes me. I'm just a figure of fun. The Nutty Noah of Norfolk according to one newspaper."

"If you don't cease this treacherous behaviour of your own accord, steps may have to be taken. You have been warned."

"Are you from the police?"

"No. I am not from the police."

"I don't trust her, Mr Rawlings. She's just like those politicians who come into the radio station and lie their heads off. I bet she's from MI5."

"Is that true?"

"In a manner of speaking."

"What sort of manner?"

"Well, it's true that MI5 was asked to intervene but, well, it's the holiday season, they're a bit short-staffed so I was asked to step in."

"So who are you?"

"I'm a local council recycling officer and I do hope your workmen will be disposing of those off-cuts and wood shavings in a responsible manner."

The Second Book of Passion

1. Put not your trust in government or officials. When threats are made and danger rears its head sleep not, but keep watch in the dark hours.

"I say, Malcolm, are you there?"

"Over here, Mags."

"I thought I'd come and keep watch with you for a while."

"I'm glad."

"Me too. Glad we're together to face…well, whatever it is we're going to face."

"Yes. Oh, Mags, I…"

"Yes, Malcolm."

"Oh, nothing."

"We might be facing the end of all life on this planet, Malcolm."

"I know."

"So if you've got something to say, best spit it out while there's still time."

"I love you, Mags."

"Oh, Malcolm. Why ever didn't you say so before?"
"I thought you'd laugh at me."
"You are a silly. Give us a cuddle."

2. I will think of them all through the watches of the night. I sing in the shadow of their wings. I will hold them safe above the waters of the deep through the strength of my timbers.

"Oh, Mags, oh Mags. Together we can look to the future."
"Which is somewhat uncertain, Malcolm."
"But at least it's interesting, Mags, and that's a damn sight better than what we had before, isn't it?"
"It certainly is, Malcolm but we must stop shilly-shallying. It's all hands on deck – and all the other bits – we have an Ark to build."

The Book of The Final Days

1. And build they did. My deck planks went on. My superstructure was…well…super. I was properly caulked – that's caulked, you understand, not corked. Then I was given a nice coat of varnish on my…Yes, well never mind. They worked well, they worked heartily…

"Think we could do with another coat of paint on the wheelhouse, Ted."
"No not like that, Malcolm. The twisty bit has to fit under the thingumyjig."
"Mind your backs, feeding trough coming through. Oof."
"Hope you don't mind me mentioning in, Vicar, but that's a very silly place to put a nail."

2. ...and the work went on. Handrails, bunk beds, store rooms, animal pens, a little row of hooks to hang sou'westers on, a sticky-up bit on top which Ted said was just decoration and I was finished.

"She's finished."

"She sure is, Mr Rawlings. One Ark, as requested. All ready to set sail when needed."

"Good. And bang on schedule."

3. And lo, even as they stood back and admired their handiwork, the windows of heaven were opened and the gentle patter of rain began to fall upon the face of the earth. And fell...and fell...

BR-Exit

It was only after our Club had folded, neighbours who were once friends no longer spoke to each other, lawsuits over the disputed ownership of some of the more specialist models were well underway and the town had come to terms with the loss of a valuable annual source of income, that we looked back and realised how easily all this could have been avoided.

The Wandleford and District Model Railway Club was first formed in 1957. Starting with just a handful of men it grew steadily over the years and by 2017 when it celebrated its Diamond Jubilee there were sixty members which was a nice match, sixty members, sixty years.

The Club not only provided an outlet for those of us who loved trains but it also provided a huge boost to the local economy. Every year since 1965, we had held a big Model Railway Exhibition in April. This had grown over the years to the point where it was attended by model railway clubs from all over the south of England. This event was much welcomed in the town as shops, hotels, pubs and restaurants all benefited from the influx of exhibitors and visitors.

Every year Selwyn Goosander, the owner of the Gormless Goose pub in the High Street, said, "I couldn't give a stuff about trains but that Model Railway Exhibition each April gets my financial year off to a flying start. More power to their driving wheels, that's what I say."

Over the years several women had also joined the club. Initially, this development was resisted by some of the older members but as they gradually died off a more realistic approach was accepted. As one younger member put it, "If women wanted to join we should let them. Women should have the right to choo-choo-choose."

This occasioned several groans but the motion was passed.

It was a happy Club. Some of us were keen on historical accuracy, some preferred to 'drive' the trains, some were expert at building scenery, and some were skilled at the mechanical side including the introduction of electronics that had gradually been increasing over the years. Some quite openly came for the social side, though were usually quite happy to act as marshals at the various exhibitions that the Club attended.

Ever since 1973, our Club had rented a small building on the edge of town which had once been a wholesale furniture business. Back then membership was steadily increasing and this gave us the space to expand as, inevitably, a large membership meant a variety of interests. Many members loved modelling steam lines from the era of British Railways pre-1948. Others loved the sleek lines of modern diesel, especially those from various European countries.

This difference wasn't a problem. We had the space, we had a wide range of skills amongst the members, so we gradually developed two areas of operation. At one end of the building, steam chugged happily along rural branch lines, while at the other end, high-speed continental trains rushed across viaducts in mountain ranges. Each group had its own dedicated members but many people ranged happily between them, so those who specialised in building scenery might spend some time lovingly creating a 1930s station building and then move on to constructing a viaduct through the Alps.

My own preference was for pre-war branch lines, like the Felixstowe branch line in Suffolk, the Somerset and Dorset railway, and the Waveney Valley Branch line. These were my passion, but I could still enjoy watching a modern diesel locomotive powering through continental scenery and I was always willing to help sort out a tricky bit of construction on either layout.

So, in spite of a range of different interests, all was harmony in the Club until around the time of our 60th anniversary when Ivor Peverell decided to put himself forward as Chairman at the forthcoming election. Ivor was a retired solicitor, with a university education but a primary school intelligence and with an arrogance that could sink a battleship. He had twice stood for election to the Town Council but had never succeeded, a fact which clearly puzzled him.

When he stood in the council elections he had been heard to say that the town needed someone like him, not just as a councillor but as its chairman. His election leaflet talked about making sure that people with money or influence would never get fined for illegal parking or speeding, a statement that even the people with money or influence found a bit too blatant for comfort.

Thwarted in his aim to become a small frog in a big pond (in local terms), he decided to become a big frog in a small pond and set his sights on the Wandleford and District Model

Railway Club. He clearly had very little interest in railway modelling, power was what he was after in whatever forum he could find it, though he shrugged off the idea that any responsibility went with it.

He did make a half-hearted attempt to interact with other members, throwing in comments about low-relief buildings, 4-6-2 locomotives and the relative merits of loose and fixed ballast, but none of us were really fooled. Still, he paid his subs and if he sounded off at great length in the bar after meetings we all thought he was a harmless clown.

How wrong we were.

Our current chairman, Willoughby Fawcett, had been in the post for over ten years. He loved all aspects of the Club, but he was now in his late eighties and, as he put it himself, "The steam has gone out of my boilers, and it's time to shunt off into a siding."

He gave us plenty of warning so we all knew that at the AGM in six months' time, we would need to find a new chairman.

However, it wasn't as simple as that. The initial problem was that the British Railways section of the Club wanted one of their members to become chairman while the Continental Railways sector was equally keen on one of theirs. Even so, it would almost certainly have been settled amicably had not Ivor Peverell stepped in.

He was nobody's first choice but in the friendly rivalry between the two sectors of the Club, he saw his chance and, like the glossy but brutal street fighter he was, set about building himself a power base. He began by siding with those modellers who concentrated on British Railways. He sang the praises of their models, and the engineering superiority of BR in general, all the time disparaging the continental modelling section. In the same way that a leakage of sewage gradually contaminates water, this soon had the effect of creating tensions between the two areas of our Club.

Ivor began by pointing out that the British Railways section of the Club was effectively subsidising the Continental section. This was not true, but a big lie said consistently will always be believed.

"That continental crowd buy in a lot of their items," he declaimed, "while we in British Railways mostly make our own. Why should our membership fees constantly subsidise them?"

Our Treasurer, Meg Fitzwilliam, tried to point out that this was not the case.

"All materials bought in are available to all members," she said, "in fact, because Hugh Dromgoole has an account with many of our suppliers, they give the Club a fifteen per cent discount on all purchases."

Hugh was actually a keen continental modeller so you would think that argument was killed stone dead but there's none so gullible as those who want to believe.

"How do we know he passes that fifteen per cent on to us?" said Darren Bigsby.

"Because I can show you the figures," said Meg but Darren wasn't interested in facts. He and Hugh had not been on speaking terms since Hugh's cat had fished a Koi Carp out of Darren's ornamental pond and had proceeded to dissect it in full view.

Having created tension where none had existed before, Ivor moved on to the next stage of his campaign. The current layout of the British Railways section had got rather bogged down and Ivor seized on this to denigrate the continental modellers still further.

"The continental model is stifling our British Railways," he proclaimed, "if we parted company from them think of all the benefits. We'd no longer be hampered by their demands on our skills, we could make much more progress on our British Railways layout, which is always the biggest attraction at exhibitions, and we would double the amount of money available to us."

Those arguments were so blatantly ridiculous that no one really took them seriously. Unfortunately, that turned out to be the problem. There will always be some people who feel disgruntled about something or other and Ivor did not find it difficult to persuade several people that they would be better off if the British Railways section existed on its own. The result was that in the months leading up to the AGM the 'Let's separate from the continentals' movement gathered momentum.

The continental modelling section did themselves no favours. They refused to take this proposal seriously. They thought that it was obvious to anyone with an IQ that reached double figures that a symbiotic relationship between the two sections of the Club brought so many benefits to all parties that no one could take this suggestion to split up seriously.

Unfortunately, ignorant prejudice and a passion for the purely imaginary 'good old days' is a difficult roller coaster to stop and Ivor's campaign began to gather support. Although Ivor himself had only enough common sense to cover a postage stamp, his instinct for publicity was not in doubt. His crowning stroke was to give his campaign a slogan – a slogan which, when often repeated, provided a lot of impetus.

"We are fighting a campaign to reclaim our national heritage," he declaimed. "We need to separate our efficient British Railways operation from the disaster of the Continental modellers. We'll call it BR-Exit."

Some of the British Railways members such as myself had no patience with such rhetoric but it went down very well with the brain-dead members of the Club (every organisation has a few of those).

Still the Continental section did very little. They simply could not believe that such a motion would ever be passed at the AGM.

But it was. The Club rules stated that only members who were physically present at the AGM could vote. Unfortunately, the outgoing chairman, Willoughby Fawcett, was not well at the time and could not be there on that evening. His deputy, Sidney Dudlose, had all the charisma of a half-eaten cold sausage and was powerless against the dynamic thrust of Ivor Peverell and his gang of BR-Exiters. Some of us tried to insist that a two-thirds majority of the vote would be required to make any fundamental changes but we were shouted down. There were 31 members at the AGM and 16 of them voted for BR-Exit so the separatist motion was carried.

Following that, Ivor Peverell raced home as the new Chairman and the future of the Club was doomed.

Ivor was triumphant. "We've got our railway back so the future is bright."

"Not completely bright," said Meg the Treasurer. "if the Continental members don't renew their membership then our income will plummet."

"Nonsense," said Ivor, "let them go if they're that petty-minded. Now that we're a proper British Railways Club again others will come flocking to join us."

Willoughby Fawcett was outraged at the outcome, especially when it emerged that several members, all continental modellers as it happened, had failed to receive their AGM notice and agenda and so had not been present.

"Slight admin error," said Ivor breezily, "their own fault for not staying in touch."

Following the AGM things started getting nasty. The new committee, all of whom licked Ivor Peverell's boots before each meeting, made it clear that the Continental Modellers were no longer welcome. Within a very short space of time, the Continental layout was dismantled and moved into storage and their members resigned from the Club.

This was greeted with cheers by the BR-Exiters until three months later when the quarterly rent on the hall became due. At the regular committee meeting, Meg Fitzwilliam asked what they wanted to do about paying the next quarter's rent.

"Stupid question," said Ivor Peverell, "pay it of course."

"What with?" asked Meg.

"Duh. Money, dumbo," said Ivor Peverell.

"Money which we don't have," said Meg, "we have less than half the membership fees that we had last year."

"That can't be right."

"If you'd looked at the figures I sent you last week," said Meg, "you'd have seen that it is right. Figures don't lie." Then she added under her voice, "They're the only thing round here that doesn't."

There was much uproar in the committee as the figures were passed around.

"Why weren't we warned about this?" Darren Bigsby asked.

"You were," said Meg, "I circulated these accounts to every member of the committee a month ago, together with my projected estimates of income and liabilities. As things stand at present we cannot go on affording the rent on this hall."

More uproar.

Ivor Peverell shouted it down. "Not a problem we'll double the membership fees until we're back on our feet. There's bound to be a few teething problems."

"Still won't be enough," said Meg, "there's also bills for all the outstanding materials and electrical component supplies. They're twice as much as last year."

"How can they be?"

"Simple," said Meg, "we no longer get big discounts from the suppliers. In their eyes, we're a much smaller operation now and anyway, all the deals were negotiated by Hugh Dromgoole and you kicked him out."

"Teething troubles," said Ivor Peverell half-heartedly but there were murmurings around the table.

"Oh, and one other thing," said Meg, "I'm resigning. I've had enough of you bunch of sycophantic morons," and she picked up her handbag and stalked out.

"Good riddance," yelled Ivor Peverell after her but several faces round the table looked glum.

The much-vaunted increase in members once the Club became 'pure' British Railways never happened. Instead, the membership began to decline especially as the membership fees continued to rise. Finally, in desperation, the committee decided it would have to sub-let the part of the hall originally used by the Continental section to gain the necessary income. Unfortunately, the only people who were interested were a group of salsa dancers. They paid their rent but the vigorous rhythm of the dancing made the floor resonate and several of the less well-made bits of scenery tended to topple over.

Then another problem occurred. Modern model railways rely heavily on electronics rather than just electrics and it turned out that those members who understood electronics had belonged to the Continental Group. Previously, of course, their expertise was available to both sections of the Club but now that was gone.

As the various electronic components developed problems that no one could solve, the Club was forced back to electric motors and controllers, many of which were now pretty old. This did not find favour with many of the members, especially the younger ones, one of whom was heard to remark.

"If we are constantly going to move backwards why don't we go the whole hog and have clockwork trains?"

The final disaster was, of course, the demise of the Annual Model Railway Exhibition. The modelling world is a small one and news of the BR-Exit disaster in our town was soon common knowledge.

Bookings for space at the hall and in the local hotels were cancelled one by one. No one, it seemed, wanted to come and exhibit in a hall which was shared with salsa dancers and where there was only one tiny layout whose control systems were failing and which was not finished anyway as the Club could not pay for materials. This was not a great attraction to more successful clubs.

The commercial outlets in the town were outraged and when Ivor Peverell tried to get a drink at the Gormless Goose, Selwyn threw him out and barred him for life.

The Club is still there but a shadow of its former self. I haven't been there for ages and I've been told that the Club layout is now a single circuit of track with a clockwork Thomas The Tank Engine trundling around it. I'm sure this is a slight exaggeration but there is nothing there for me anymore.

What I do know is that something that gave a lot of people a lot of pleasure and which brought benefits to our town was destroyed by arrogance, personal greed, stupidity and an artificial nostalgia.

Rumour has it that Ivor Peverell has turned his attention to the golf club. I hope they take note of our experience or they'll be reduced to a putting green before you can say "Fore."

The Blues in Black and White

It was the colours that caught my eye first and after that, I noticed the people themselves. The stark contrast of their clothes, nothing but black and white, made them stand out like a football on a cricket pitch among the more conventionally dressed people in the art gallery café.

I tried not to look at them too obviously as I toyed with my extremely expensive salad but I found it impossible to look away. The woman's skirt was jet black, her blouse black and white check, her hat which might have been nailed onto her skull as it never shifted, was also black. Her stockings were white, her shoes black and she wore a white wrap around her rather bony shoulders. She looked rather like an upright zebra.

She was, I guessed, probably in her mid to late thirties. She sat without moving, gazing straight ahead, seemingly not conscious of the crowds around her. She was unusual enough in herself but on her lap she held a baby, maybe five, six, seven months old. The baby, like its mother, if it was its mother, sat perfectly still. It didn't fidget, or cry, or gaze around it. It just sat, motionless and like its mother, if it was its mother, it was dressed totally in black and white. White booties, black leggings, a white top and a black beanie pulled low over its ears as if it were in early training to become a football hooligan.

If the pair hadn't been so visually arresting I would have turned away at once, maybe even shifted my chair so I could no longer see the child on the woman's lap. But the whole thing was somehow depersonalised, almost as though the figures were an art tableau which should have been in one of the galleries rather than in the café with its atmosphere of cooking and damp raincoats.

The man sitting next to the woman was clearly older. His face was long and thin, he was clean-shaven and his hair was just starting to recede a little. Although he, too, was also dressed entirely in black and white, it looked less strange on him. Black shoes, black trousers, white shirt, black jacket, black tie. I thought I caught a glimpse of a white sock below the trouser leg but I couldn't be sure without making it obvious that I was watching them.

In some ways I was glad of the distraction. I had only come to the gallery by chance. I knew I had to get out of the house. I had to do something, anything. Shopping hadn't worked, just walking the streets hadn't worked. I'd considered a film but realised that sitting on my own in the dark was inviting trouble but then I saw a poster for this exhibition and so I had come here to spend an hour looking at pictures and sculptures before suddenly realising I was hungry. And now there was this…enigma.

I pecked at another piece of salmon which was rather dry and continued to watch the black and white couple surreptitiously. It wasn't just the unusual bleakness of their clothes that puzzled me, it was the immobility.

I wondered if they too had been around the exhibition. If they too had been moved by the beauty of some of it and the banality of the rest as I had been. Perhaps, like me, they had reached art overload and had retreated here to eat and regroup. Possible, of course, but somehow I doubted it. There was something in their immobility, their isolation from the world around them and from each other, that made me doubt it was art that had brought them here. Or maybe it was just me, my own misery and isolation projected onto them.

I had not realised until recently that isolation is a state of mind, not a physical experience. You can feel totally isolated in a newly decorated room that will never fulfil its planned function and you can feel just as isolated in the middle of a large crowd.

In many ways being alone in a large crowd is harder. It emphasises the realisation that there is no escape. I wanted to get up and go, abandon my tasteless salmon, and return to my lonely misery. But this chequerboard-clad couple fascinated me. I could not take my eyes off them.

And then their food arrived, large plates piled high. Knowing what I had paid for a rather modest salmon salad I realised that their meal must have cost a lot of money. As the plates went down in front of them there was the first sign of movement. They both glanced down but made no attempt to start on their meal. They did not look at each other at all or exchange any remarks. Finally, the man picked up a fork in a rather desultory way and made a few minor forays into the food on his plate. The woman and the baby didn't move.

And then there was another diversion. A young woman, maybe in her twenties, appeared at the door of the restaurant. She glanced around and then made a beeline for the couple I had been watching. She was clearly from somewhere in the Far East, possibly Filipino, and she was propelling a pushchair in front of her. I use the word 'pushchair' in the generic sense. Probably these days it would be called a baby buggy but what a buggy. It oozed expense, curved hood, padded arms, white handle, and black straps. For all I knew it had its own SatNav buried under the cushion.

The young girl arrived at the table. She neither spoke to the couple nor was she acknowledged. She parked the buggy, applied some kind of brake and then leaned forward and took the baby off the woman's lap. The baby, passive as ever, allowed itself to be placed in the buggy and was quickly and efficiently strapped in.

The woman continued to sit for a moment then, without glancing at the man beside her or the young woman and the baby, she too picked up her knife and fork and ate a few mouthfuls of food.

The whole situation seemed very bizarre. I could hardly take my eyes off this rather strange tableau but when I glanced around the restaurant to see if anyone else was watching there were no signs that they were. The rest of the room seemed perfectly normal, people coming and going, the light buzz of conversation, food being brought to tables and used crockery removed. It was as though the group I was watching, together with myself, were in some kind of bubble in time.

The woman and the man continued to eat but very slowly as though they weren't quite sure what they were meant to be doing. They still didn't look at each other and every move they made seemed laboured and lethargic. In contrast, now that the baby was firmly imprisoned in the buggy, the young woman began to feed it with a speed and vigour that was quite startling, especially in contrast to the baby's parents, if they were its parents.

The young woman had produced a jar, presumably some kind of baby food, and was spooning it into the baby's mouth. The baby was clearly used to this process because, although its body remained as static as ever, its mouth opened and closed with extreme rapidity. It needed to, there was no delay in the process. Mouth open, spoon in, mouth shut, spoon into the jar, mouth open, spoon in. It had the efficiency of a well-oiled production line.

Before long the jar was empty but, to my surprise, another jar was immediately opened and the whole business began again. For the first time I realised just how big this baby was. It had all the usual baby features, and I saw no reason to doubt my original estimate of its age, but there was a roundness to it, a puffiness almost, that suddenly seemed to me to be very unbecoming.

At this point I looked away. Seeing a couple with a baby was hard enough but a baby that seemed to be more of a caricatured accessory than a loved and cherished being was more than I could bear. I concentrated on my food and several minutes passed before I looked across at the family, if it was a family, again.

Feeding was obviously finished, at least as far as the baby was concerned. The young woman was wiping its face, a process it endured without any protest. The cloth she was using I noticed, by now without any surprise, was black and white check. In contrast, the woman and the man, both still staring straight ahead, were not making a lot of progress with their food.

When the baby wiping was finished the young woman checked that it was properly strapped into its buggy, produced a blanket (yes, of course, it was a black and white blanket), from the carrier hanging on the back of the buggy and tucked it in securely around the baby. Then she stood up, took off the brake and, without a single glance at the woman and man beside her, and without a word being exchanged between them, she pushed the buggy across the restaurant and out of the door.

It was one of the strangest things I have ever seen but as far as I could see no one else had noticed anything at all. I shook my head to try and clear it. Was this really happening? Was I having some kind of vision?

I took a casual look back at the couple still toying with their food and then almost did a double take. They were still sitting there, motionless apart from an occasional poke at their plate, but suddenly to my horror, I realised that there were tears running down the face of the woman and splashing onto her plate. I looked at the man. He wasn't crying but his eyes were tight shut and his face screwed up as though he were fighting to keep himself under control.

I glanced away quickly. I felt as though I had intruded into someone's personal space, seeing something no one else was meant to see. Part of me wanted to go over to them, put my arm around the woman's shoulders, and try and comfort her, but I knew that any action like that was impossible. I had no doubt in my mind that she was undergoing a moment of deep despair but, as I knew only too well, such moments have to be faced alone. No one, no matter how close, no matter how loving, can reach you at times like this. The most they can do is to keep you from harm while you work your way through your own personal hell.

When I risked another look I saw that they were both getting up from the table, most of their food untouched. Their movements were mechanical, they still did not speak. They did not even glance down at the table to see if they had inadvertently forgotten anything as most of us do when leaving a restaurant. They turned to go and then it happened.

The man already had his back to me but as the woman turned there was a split second when her eyes met mine and she knew. I knew she knew. We recognised each other's pain. For one long moment, I thought she was going to speak but instead, she just shook her head, made a small gesture of despair and turned to follow her husband, if it was her husband, as they headed towards the door.

I watched them go. The room was long with windows spaced down each side. As the woman and man in their black and white clothing passed from the window lights into the darker areas and back into the light, bits of them seemed to appear and disappear like an uncompleted jigsaw. It was as though their component parts were all moving separately, perhaps to come together as a whole outside the building.

Or perhaps not.

They vanished from my sight. I felt drained and as I turned back to my own despair I felt the first tears begin to drip onto the remains of my very expensive salad.

The Reunion

My first thought is surprise at the amount of increase in stomachs and the corresponding decrease in hair. Do I look like this too? No, I can't; but it is hard to believe that I was ever a boy with this group of men in their sixties. It's over 40 years since I have seen most of them and on first showing, I would be quite happy if it were another 40 before I did so again. I catch Roger's eye and see his eyebrows go up and we instinctively head for the bar.

When the invitation arrived my first reaction was to chuck it in the bin – metaphorically that is, as it actually came by email. To be fair I had been given advance warning. My first wife, Susan, had rung up one day to say she'd had a call from someone called Victor Sponge who asked for me. As she and I had parted some 25 years earlier this was rather a surprise to her but he said he had got her name from another old friend who had lost touch with me but still had her number. He explained that he had been at school with me and that next summer it would be fifty years since one hundred and twenty little boys in grey shorts, all with 11 plus passes, had gathered in the playground of Palmerston School in south London to begin our grammar school lives. He was, apparently, so moved by this memory that he had decided to try and contact the other 119 and arrange a 50-year reunion.

I have remarried but Susan and I are good friends and I could hear the hint of laughter in her voice as she passed on this message.

"Sounds like a lot of fun," she said. "Will you be wearing the little grey shorts again? If so, please do send me a picture."

I thought back over the seven years I had spent at Palmerston, years which on the whole I would rather forget. There was no doubt in my mind that any successes I might have achieved in my life were in spite of, rather than because of, that school. There is only one boy – well, man – from that time with whom I was still in touch and then only infrequently. The rest I could hardly remember and Victor Sponge rang no memory at all.

"Why the hell would I want to go to something like that?" I asked.

"No idea," said Susan, "but I promised to ring him back when I'd spoken to you. What do you want me to tell him? Shall I give him your number?"

I thought for a moment. "No," I said at last, "give him my email. I'll see what he's got to say but keep him at arm's length for the moment."

After she had rung off I thought back to my schooldays. Contrary to popular myth they were not the happiest days of my life. In fact, I had hated every minute at least until I reached the 6th form. With hindsight, it was hardly surprising. The school was pretentious – a Latin grace so long that the food was cold before it was done, a Latin school song, a system of prefects and sub-prefects whose only apparent purpose was to justify official bullying, a House cup system whose main object seemed to be to provide a reason for pouring scorn on the losers, in fact, all the bollocks of a Billy Bunter novel which had no place in the early 1960s. There was no attempt – or none that I remembered – to explain why you had to learn something, only the insistence that you did and if you didn't you would be beaten. They had a lot to learn about motivation, the masters who ran that school.

Had I been academically brilliant (which I wasn't), or good at team games (which I wasn't) or joined the Combined Cadet Force (which I didn't), life might have been bearable. As it was all I remembered was harsh rules, difficult homework, bad teaching, many punishments and a longing for the final bell at ten to four.

But perhaps most of all I remembered Kevin Chilcott, the stocky, wiry boy who made my first two years a misery. Anyone who tells you that bullying at school is just high spirits and part of the natural order of growing up is either a liar or a fantasist. For whatever reason, Kevin Chilcott took a dislike to me and as he was quite a powerful boy and I was anything but, I always came off worse.

It began with all the usual schoolboy torments; gripping my shoulders while he kneed me violently in the thigh to give me a dead leg, Chinese burns on the wrist, and half-nelsons with my arm up my back. But that was only starters. As that first year progressed he would leap on me from behind, forcing me to the ground where he would either rub my nose in the mud, or turn me over and, pinning my shoulders down with his knees, grind his fist into my face. He would punch me in the soft part of my upper arm and all the time he would be snarling – I can't think of another word for it – telling me how useless I was, a weed, a waste of space.

In my 11-year-old dreams, I imagined meeting Kevin Chilcott on a dark night and driving over him in a tank or pushing him over a cliff or into a vat of boiling oil. The fact that I couldn't drive a tank, that we were miles from the sea and I wouldn't have the faintest idea where one could acquire a vat of boiling oil, didn't make any difference. I wanted to hurt him, I wanted to see him suffer. I wanted revenge.

Looking back with the eyes of an adult I cannot believe I just put up with it but as an 11-year-old – and a young one at that – I didn't know what to do. Telling one of the masters was pointless. Not only were they all remote and unapproachable but I knew deep down that there was nothing they could do. Even if they believed me (unlikely) and tried to do something (even more unlikely) they could not be there all the time and I knew that Kevin Chilcott's revenge would be swift and severe.

It ended, of course, as all torments end. We moved on up the school, found ourselves in different forms, other activities took over and the bullying stopped. I haven't thought about it for years but when this reunion was proposed and I let my thoughts return to that school the prominent memory was the misery of those first few terms. Not just Kevin Chilcott himself, but the pain and the humiliation and the feeling of powerlessness.

I never let those two years of vicious bullying blight my life, in fact, I thought I'd forgotten all about them, but now with the offer of a school reunion in front of me I find, slightly to my surprise, that my anger and resentment towards Kevin Chilcott is as strong as ever.

It's not a nice thing to admit but I found myself hoping that he'd had a miserable life, perhaps been involved in a bad car accident, perhaps stricken down by some kind of disease, perhaps caught with his hand in the till and had been disgraced. Anything that would have made him as miserable as he had made me.

These are not comfortable thoughts but I realise how intense they are. Maybe I should go to this reunion, maybe it's time to face my tormentor, maybe this will be my chance to exact some kind of revenge. The tank and boiling oil still aren't an option but maybe I could trip him up at the top of the stairs or 'accidentally' pour my beer all down his front. Anything to hurt him or humiliate him would, even now after all these years, give me great satisfaction.

Roger and I are at the bar now and two pints of beer are being pushed towards us. We each take a good long drink and look around us. A room full of strangers, people first met when our lives were just beginning, now all heading towards retirement. One surprise is the number of women in the crowd. Wives, presumably, maybe girlfriends or mistresses, but what sense of loyalty or boredom persuaded them to come is beyond me.

I appreciate that any memory I might have retained for any of these people is forty years old so it's not surprising I don't recognise anyone and if we haven't bothered to stay in touch after all this time why the hell are we trying now?

"Was this a good idea?" I ask.

"Probably not," says Roger, "but the beer's not bad."

"Just as well," I say, "I think we're going to need a lot of it."

The reunion is being held at the Old Palmerstonians Club House about 3 miles from the school. It is the first time I have ever been here, a refusal to join the Old Boys Association being the last of my rebellions when I finally escaped into the real world. It is a handsome room, well decked out in wooden panelling and through the window I can see a balcony overlooking the rugger or cricket pitch, depending on the season.

For a brief moment – very brief – a surge of fictional nostalgia wells up in me. In another life, in another age, I could have belonged here, a successful school career behind me, one-time captain of cricket, whiling away the summer afternoons in this clubhouse with my contemporaries watching a spectacular spin bowler do his stuff from the wheelie bins end. But no, not really. That kind of fantasy belongs in 1950s schoolboy story land and anyway, looking around at this collection of elderly paunches, not a very likely one either.

We've all been given name badges and photos of us when we were 11, taken presumably from a school photo that mad Victor Sponge has dug up from somewhere. Maybe he raided the school archive, surely he wouldn't have kept it from all those years ago. Would he? Well, given his tireless enthusiasm for this event, he just might have done.

Roger and I split up to cruise through the crowd separately. Although he and I were – and still are – friends, he left the school after the 4th form and moved away from the area. In any case, we were in separate forms and separate houses so will not necessarily remember the same people.

Rather to my surprise, quite a number of names have been coming back to me since the invitation first arrived. Names, not always with faces, of people who were bearable company for a term or two until the swirling waters of school life carried us off in different directions. Paul Webster who had the statistics of every 1st and 2nd division football match since the war in his head, Norman Rottinger who had a passion for art and later, in the 6th form, first introduced me to surrealist painting, Graham Sparrow – a fast bowler to be reckoned with, Martin 'Tubby' Franklin who everyone said smelt, though he probably didn't, Olly Jenkins, supercilious with a pointy nose and who never used one word when twelve would do.

When Victor Sponge's email arrived I let it lie for some days. My first instinct was to indulge in a stream of invective, get some of the long-buried hatred of that school off my chest so to speak, but then it wasn't Victor's fault that I'd been so unhappy there. He clearly had very different memories – or was having a very dull adult life – so if he wanted to organise a reunion then why shouldn't he? After all, I didn't have to go. Several times I went to the keyboard to tap out a refusal but always stopped short. In the end, I picked up the phone and rang Roger.

"I bet I know what you're calling about," were his opening words.

"Ah, so you've had one too."

"Sure have. So are you going?"

"Can't think why I'd want to bother."

"Nor me…but…"

"What sort of 'but'?"

"Don't know. But where's the harm, I suppose."

"It was another life, Roger."

"Yes, I know, but…"

I sighed. Perhaps a sense of curiosity kicked in. "Tell you what, I'll go if you go. If we go together we might get by. Haven't seen you for a while anyway."

"Okay, it's a deal."

And so we have come. A warm Saturday in September. It's good to see Roger but as we walk through the door and some woman – presumably a wife, perhaps even Mrs Victor Sponge – gives us a name badge, I begin to think of all the things I'd rather be doing. In some way, I'm worried in case my presence here is proof that I think this is a good idea.

I, circulate, beer in hand, almost like a passport, a reason to be in this crowd. One or two faces seem vaguely familiar but it is usually only by peering at their badge, as they are peering at mine, do we add names to faces. I meet Norman Rottinger and for the sake of something to say tell him how he first introduced me to the work of Salvador Dali which has given me so much pleasure over the years. He seems surprised. I have a brief chat with Brian Hitchman who I remember as being passionate about the Air Corps. He is now married to a Latvian woman called Aija who for some unaccountable reason has come with him. They now live in Riga where he works for a plumbing firm. Graham Sparrow looking decidedly ravaged, with a red face, prominent veins, huge beer belly. It'd be some time since he last bowled a yorker.

Keith Stainton, Derek Turner, Patrick Maloney they come and they go – the "go" is the best bit. Then suddenly I see him on the far side of the room. Kevin Chilcott. At least I think it's him. It's nothing like the 12-year-old face that is burned into my brain but I recognise the way this man nods his head forward and sideways when making a point, a gesture I had plenty of time to record in my memory as I lay flat on the ground, his knees pressing down on my shoulders, his fist grinding into my nose or squeezing the muscles in my upper arm until I squealed with pain. I see again the look of glee on his face as he hurt me physically while verbally informing me what a useless waste of space I was. Kevin Chilcott. And now, suddenly, all the hatred comes tumbling back. I want to leap across the floor and smash his face against the wall.

I am surprised at the depth of feeling still there after all this time.

The Chairman of the Old Palmerstonians, a man I have never seen in my life before, pings on a glass and calls us to order. He proposes a toast to the "*the Class of 1961*" as he puts it, been watching too much American TV if you ask me, then we all sit down to eat.

I hardly notice the food that is put in front of me. All my thoughts are of Kevin Chilcott. I entertain wild fancies of him having a heart attack there in front of us all, or of him choking on his food and while people rush to help him I manage to get in the way so he is not helped and he dies.

"Oh, please," I think, "grow up. That's only one stage removed from a vat of boiling oil."

The meal ends, more drinks are bought and the circulating begins again. Roger appears at my elbow.

"Think we've done our duty, don't you? Shall we get out of here?"

"In a moment."

I push my way through the crowd looking for Kevin Chilcott. Before long I spot him and I catch up with him at the head of the stairs that lead down to the cloakrooms.

As I reach him he turns and faces me. "Oh, hallo…" His voice is rather thin and quavery. He leans forward and peers at my name badge. "Such a long time ago, wasn't it. I'm afraid I don't remember you at all."

I am stunned. You don't remember? You knocked several kinds of hell out of me for the best part of two years and you don't remember?

I feel the hatred welling up in me. I want to hit him pummel him, kick him in the groin. Anything to give him pain.

But then he smiles and, unbelievably, holds out his hand. "So much water under the bridge. Were we friends at school?"

I feel my fists clench and then suddenly, as he continues to smile, I don't see the snarling bulk of an 11-year-old pushing my face into the grass. I see a tired-looking 61-year-old, overweight, stooped, with red lines on his cheeks, and thinning hair and suddenly all my hatred seems pointless.

I reach out and take his proffered hand. "No," I say, "we weren't particular friends at school."

"Though not, but there were so many of us back then, weren't there? And it's fifty years ago. Amazing. Anyway, nice to see you again."

And he smiles and walks off.

I go and find Roger. "Come on, let's get out of here."

He looks at me. "Are you all right? What's happened?"

"Nothing," I say, "but I think I've just laid a ghost to rest."

He looks at me for a moment, then grins. "Come on, let's go and find a decent pub."

The Day Granny's Vulture Had Hiccups

I think my grandmother was probably the most wonderful woman I have ever met. I never knew my grandfather, Sailor Joe, but I adored Granny Bidsmead as she was universally known. She had huge inner strength and if I have achieved anything in my life, she was the inspiration for it. I was devastated when the Council effectively killed her in the 1990s but she certainly gave them a run for their money.

I am now in my early fifties and before it's too late I want to record an account of that amazing, although ultimately sad, Confrontation (with a capital C) between Granny Bidsmead and the Council (with another capital C). Granny herself would not have embraced the Women's Lib movement but I suspect she thought women seeking equality with men was a backward step.

My memories of Granny Bidsmead are all centred on that amazing house, number 13 Jubilee Avenue, Copley. Of course, if you visit Copley today you won't find Jubilee Avenue. Where it once stood is now a series of long curving concrete ramps connecting the town with the busy arterial road from London to Southend.

My grandmother and Sailor Joe moved out of East London and onto the Essex Marshes in the early 1920s. After the First World War land was cheap so they bought up several plots and built on them. In fact, Sailor Joe built all the houses in Jubilee Avenue and made a nice profit by doing so, but he reserved a double plot – number 13 – where he built a small house for himself and Granny.

Number 13 did not stay small for long. Granny and Joe had seven sons – five of whom became skilled tradesmen. The exceptions were Ronnie who went into the Merchant Navy and Edwin, the youngest who became a solicitor. Over the years the other boys all added a little bit to the house, always to their mother's strict specification and so by the time I first went there Number 13 stood alone – in every sense of the word. It was a large detached house of unusual character but to Granny Bidsmead it was home where she lived with two of her sons, Frank and Herbert, both knocking on a bit by the time I knew them, plus a flock of geese, a three-legged goat called Maggie, a dog without a name, eleven guinea pigs at the last count (the randy little buggers are constantly increasing), and Big V.

I think I first visited Jubilee Avenue when I was around five or six years old and my memory is of a warm and welcoming place full of excitement. To a child, the daughter of a solicitor growing up in a Birmingham suburb, this house on the edge of the Essex marshes filled with animals and individuality was an experience beyond words.

I was wary of the geese, was curious about the goat – how did it manage with only three legs – but I loved the dog and the guinea pigs. However, it was Big V who captured my heart. I had never seen anything like her, fierce and ugly and brooding, but somehow I was never afraid.

Big V was a Lappet-Faced Vulture that Granny's son, Ronnie, had brought back as a fledgling from a trip to Saudi Arabia in 1953. When Big V and Granny Bidsmead first met they took one look at each other and knew they had each found a kindred spirit. Looking back, now that I'm grown up, I do wonder about the legality of keeping a Lappet-Faced Vulture in a house in Essex, but that was not the sort of thing you would ever want to raise with Granny Bidsmead.

And so these two old birds formed a partnership, Granny inside the house and Big V roosting in the oak tree outside and coming indoors for meals. Granny Bidsmead spoke to Big V a lot and, to family and friends, it often seemed that Big V spoke back.

Big V loved to sit on the back of Granny's rocking chair or sometimes she would perch on the edge of the table uttering squawks or yelps during family discussions. Old lady and old vulture seemed to take strength from each other and Big V was accepted as perfectly normal by everyone who came to 13 Jubilee Avenue.

Granny was perfectly happy and had planned to stay in this house for the rest of her days but the Council had other ideas. It was the early nineties – the era when the term 'Green Belt' meant little more than a way of keeping trousers up for a member of a fringe political party. Jubilee Avenue was in the way of a new arterial road so a compulsory purchase order plip-plopped onto the doormat.

Granny's immediate response was to use several words that old ladies shouldn't know. Then she got down to business. She talked at great length with her son Edwin (the solicitor who was also my dad), had long and meaningful discussions with Big V and bought a shotgun. Regardless of anything the Council said, Granny Bidsmead had decided to stay put.

Of course, she was actually in a privileged position. She had absolutely no right on her side when it came to the law, but a hell of a lot going for her when it came to public sympathy. But probably her strongest card was her age. At 93 she could not have very long to go, so what was there to stop her holding out indefinitely?

And holding out was what she had every intention of doing.

I was a teenager when the great Confrontation (with a capital C) happened but I have spoken to lots of people who were around at that time and, together with my own memories I've pieced together some of the story. I'm thinking of calling it "*The Temptations Of Granny Bidsmead.*"

One of my main sources of information has been Arthur Potts. Arthur was the Area Highways Engineer at the time of the Confrontation (with a capital C) and grew up in Copley. He had known Granny Bidsmead since he was a child and was anxious to find a solution to keep everyone happy. His was the first temptation – Money. He offered her increased compensation, a new house, unlimited bottles of Guinness, and luxury for the rest of her life – all very tempting at 93.

"But your grandmother was having none of it," said Arthur when we met in the Weasel and Toadstool pub. "She just sat there with Big V perched on the back of her chair while the destruction of Jubilee Avenue crashed around her."

"So they actually started destroying Jubilee Avenue while she was still living there?"

"Indeed, they did," said Arthur. "I was with Granny B the day the clearance started. I can remember our conversation as if it were yesterday."

"Hang on a tick," I said, "I want to record this?"

I clicked the icon on my Smartphone and set it on the table between us.

Arthur took a long swig of beer and sat back in his chair. "It was quite a day. I'd barely said hello to Granny and Big V when there came a huge crash and the sound of tinkling glass."

I moved the phone a bit closer to him, anxious not to miss a word.

"They've started, I said, there goes number two."

"No, that's number three," said Granny, "number two didn't have a conservatory."

"I know they didn't. But they were starting at number two."

"Then they changed their minds. I distinctly heard the tinkling of a crumbling conservatory. Didn't we, Big V?"

Big V offered vocal agreement.

"Ouch. Does she have to squawk right in my ear?"

"Now, now, Arthur. No sulking. It's not Big V's fault that we're in this position."

"No, it's yours."

"Stuff and nonsense. All I'm doing is sitting in my own home minding my own business."

"It isn't your home. It's the council's."

"Sailor Joe and I bought this land in 1922 when it was just part of the marshes. Council did nothing with it – except empty sewage all over it. My family built this house with their own hands. I have the deeds. This land and this house are mine."

"Not since the council served the compulsory purchase order, they're not."

"Haven't seen any compulsory wotsit."

"Oh, yes, you have. It was delivered here. Recorded delivery."

"Vulture ate it."

"Try telling that to the council."

"I'm not telling it to anybody. None of their business. I ain't responsible for what Big V eats."

"How do you know she ate it if you never saw it?"

"Stands to reason. She was a bit off-colour for days. Appalling indigestion. She never gets taken bad with telephone bills."

Listening to Arthur I must confess I had some sympathy for him. I knew that arguing with my grandmother was a bit like trying to empty Niagara with a teaspoon.

"Mrs Bidsmead, it is only because of the greatest respect I have for you that I persuaded the Council Highways Committee to let me try and gently reason with you."

"Cobblers. You're scared stiff, Arthur. Sticks out a mile. Be cross with you, won't they, if you have to trot back and say the old bat ain't gonna budge. Because I ain't, Arthur. This is our home and this is where we stay. Isn't it Big V?"

"Ouch. She bit my ear."

"Mere nibble because she likes you. And you like her too, don't you, Arthur?"

"Well…"

"'Course you do, you're our friend. She doesn't let everyone stroke her feathers."

"Well, the yeast tablets have certainly worked wonders. I haven't seen her plumage shine like that for a long time."

"You ought to try them yourself, Arthur. You're going a bit thin on top. Not wearing too well, my lad, eh?"

"Mrs Bidsmead, I am here on a serious matter. We are not talking about the Council trying to scrump your apples…"

"They'd be hard-pressed to be as good as you were, Arthur."

There was a pause and I saw Arthur smile to himself, reliving happy memories no doubt.

"It's very kind of you to say so. I always felt I showed a certain flair for those kinds of operations."

"You worked up a nice line in diversionary tactics as I recall."

"Bangers left over from firework night thrown into the far side of the orchard…"

"Young Elsie being bribed with gobstoppers to fall down outside my front door and burst into tears…"

"While I got the apples."

"Only sometimes."

"True, and now here we are again. Only this time you can't win. Please believe me, Mrs Bidsmead. I am here with a gentle approach. There will be those who follow after whose only thought will be to steamroller over any opposition, be it house, ditch, old lady or vulture."

"Old? Who you calling old? You've upset me, Arthur. Think yourself lucky that I don't put you over my knee."

"Mrs Bidsmead, I am 58."

"That's no excuse for being rude. I trust that when you grow up you'll learn that respect for your elders costs nothing."

"Can we get back to the by-pass, please?"

"Of course. I didn't realise you had to go. Off you trot then and mind out when you cross the road. Look both ways, won't you."

"Mrs Bidsmead, please. Don't you understand? They are going to get you out. And it's no use squawking in my ear like that, Big V. You can't win."

"Oh, I don't know. Hang on a tick…There. What do you think of that, Arthur? Bought it the other day. Been saving up my pension."

Even all these years later Arthur was clearly shaken by the memory.

"I think two barrels are enough, don't you? The man in the shop didn't stock machine guns."

"Er…may I ask."

"Just open the window for me, Arthur, there's a good boy."

"Oh, yes, of course. It is a bit warm in here, isn't it?"

"Frankly I'm bloody freezing but I don't want to damage anything."

Sitting in the saloon bar of the Weasel and Toadstool Arthur shakily put his glass down on the table.

"And then she fired it. Both barrels. Straight out the window. Hell of a shock, not just to me but to the geese as well."

"Granny fired a shotgun?"

"She did and then she turned to me and said…"

"Damn. I'd forgotten the geese. They're not used to the noise yet. I haven't had enough practice."

"You wouldn't use that thing. Would you? My God, I believe you would."

"Can be very lonely here at night, Arthur. Set well back from the High Street, on the edge of the marshes. You wouldn't want a poor old lady left defenceless, would you?"

"Defenceless?"

"Well, that's how I put it to the nice young policeman."

"You do have a licence then?"

"Of course I do, Arthur. It would be illegal not to have a licence."

"Had it crossed your mind, Mrs Bidsmead, with all due respect, that it could be considered illegal to blast council officials and building construction workers with a 12-bore shotgun?"

"You've been watching too much television, Arthur. You're acquiring a nasty mind."

Arthur drained his glass and shook his head in disbelief.

"She was a one-off, your grandmother. She wouldn't listen to reason, not from any of us."

"And we all tried, didn't we, Arthur?"

"We did. It was like them Temptation things, just as it says in the Bible."

"What sort of temptations?"

"Well, let me see…There was four of them. I'd tried tempting her with Money – no chance. Then there was that social worker, Anna something, I think. She tried the temptation of Popularity. She pointed out that the new road might inconvenience a few locals but it will do a lot of good for a lot of people. Granny wouldn't want to spoil things for others, would she?"

"But Granny wouldn't listen."

"The real problem was that Anna – true to her vocation – was trying to protect the poor old lady from the nasty rough men. She hadn't worked out that it was the men who needed protecting from the old lady."

"So Popularity failed. What was next?"

"Nostalgia. They actually sent a young police constable, Jason Smith to deliver a court order but he didn't want to do it. He was a local lad, he'd known Granny all his life, so he glossed over the court order and tried the temptation of Nostalgia. He had a romantic view of the '*good old days*' and didn't want her to let the present spoil the past."

"Bet that went down well."

"Lead balloon time. The trouble was that it was Jason's nostalgia, not Granny's."

"I see. You mean Granny wasn't interested in the past, she just wanted to keep her own house, the house her boys had built for her, even if she ended up surrounded by concrete."

"That's about it."

"So what was the final temptation?"

"Fame."

"Fame?"

"Yes. This was down to Homer Hatton, one of the bulldozer drivers. He'd taken a great shine to Granny and told her she'd be a hero for defying the establishment. But even he wanted her to leave, eventually. His kind of heroes needed to be dragged screaming from the rubble to make them martyrs. Granny, as a winner, wasn't what he had in mind. He did enjoy a glass or two of her homemade wine though, especially the beetroot and hazel nut as I recall."

I shuddered at the mention of Granny's wine.

"But none of the temptations worked. She wouldn't budge?"

"No."

I sat silent for a moment, nursing my flavoured tonic water, going back through my own memories.

Finally, I said, "That wasn't the last temptation, Arthur. The final one was Love."

"Love?"

"Yes. Love, perhaps the most subtle temptation of all and it was offered by me. I knew that one of Granny's big fears was what would happen to Big V if she died first, so I told her I'd get my dad to find Big V a private enclosure, complete with a rocking chair, in a zoo or wildlife park somewhere. I also pointed out that all the dust and disturbance wasn't good for vultures. So I said, 'For Big V's sake, won't you come out, Granny?'"

"Didn't work."

"'Course not."

"Pity, in the light of what eventually happened."

"Yes…"

We shared a moment of silent sadness.

"She was a real fighter, wasn't she, my Granny?"

"She was that. I think my favourite memory is when she came face to face with Sidney Wilkins."

"Who was he?"

"Ah, well now, Sidney Wilkins was the project manager for Grimalkin Construction. He was worried sick that if that job went wrong he could end up building ornamental roundabouts instead of the bridge over the Channel which was his lifelong dream."

"He didn't have much judgement then."

"None at all. He simply couldn't believe that one old lady could stand between him and his project and as he got more and more desperate he alternated between cajolery and threats. I did my best to play peacemaker but…"

"You were on a hiding to nothing."

"I was. By now number 13 stood alone, surrounded by flattened houses and builders' machinery. I'd gone back to Granny B for one last-ditch attempt to make her see reason when we were interrupted by a cacophony of cackling. Scared the hell out of me."

Arthur gave a sad smile at the memory. "I remember I yelled, 'What the hell's that…?' And your grandmother replied. 'Only the geese. Must be someone at the door. Sounds like Sejanus has got someone pinned down at the gate'."

I checked the recording was still running then asked. "Sejanus, Arthur? Who was Sejanus?"

"Exactly what I asked at the time. She was full of surprises, your Granny. She looked at me as if I was a sandwich short of a picnic."

"Sejanus is the gander, Arthur. Keeps the rest in order."

"Why Sejanus?"

"Dunno really. Just liked the name. Saw it in a school programme on the telly. You ever watch them? They're good. I'm learning Portuguese, you know."

Arthur was clearly getting very stressed by these memories so I went and got him another pint with a scotch chaser. As an afterthought, I added a pack of hedgehog and dill crisps. I stuck to flavoured tonic water, determined not to miss a word of this story.

Arthur downed the scotch in one go, took a mouthful of crisps and then turned back to his pint.

"Sorry about that. It was a very stressful time."

"Of course, but was there someone at the door?"

"There was someone at the door but by the time we got there Sejanus, wings outstretched, had him pinned up against the hedge. Unfortunately, it was Sidney Wilkins and at once I knew trouble was coming. I rescued him from Sejanus, smoothed him down and then I took him indoors to effect the proper introductions."

Arthur sighed at the memory.

"Mrs Bidsmead, this is Mr Wilkins of the Grimalkin Construction Open Brackets Concrete Close Brackets Company Limited."

Mr Wilkins gave the oily smile of a lying politician. "Good morning, Mrs Bidsmead."

"Two pennorth of nothing, isn't he?"

"I beg your pardon?"

"Not much of him for someone with so many brackets."

"They're not his brackets. They're his company's."

"Oh, that explains it then. Council worker, is he, Arthur?"

"I am not a council workman, madam."

"Mr Wilkins is a Project Engineer."

"Fancy. All that and still frightened of a harmless little goose."

"Madam, I have come to tell you…"

"I am not a madam. I am not running a brothel. Fancy a glass of wine, do you? It's been a good year for the dandelion and radish."

"To hell with your bloody wine."

"Oh, now, Mr Winkleplum. You may be the bee's knees at building concrete gnomes or whatever it is you make, but you shouldn't be rude about my wine when Big V's around."

"Big V?"

"Um…It's the vulture, Mr Wilkins. On the back of that chair."

"I can see where it is, Potts. Where, I can understand. It's why that defeats me."

"She's a wine connoisseur, is Big V. Particularly fond of the rabbit and tomato vintage."

"Mrs Bidsmead, perhaps if Mr Wilkins and I came back a little later…"

"Then there's the acorn and nettle. That always goes down well."

"Perhaps tomorrow would be a better…"

Mr Wilkins was running out of patience. "Mrs Bidsmead, you are going to have to move."

"Oh, is that the time? Yes, you're right. It's getting late. Bye-bye, Mr Wimple. Nice to have met you."

"But…"

"Big V will see you out, Mr Wagglesnitch. You'll have another chance to have a gander at the gander."

Sitting in the pub I couldn't help myself. I burst out laughing. "And did he go, this Wilkins bloke?"

"Oh, yes, he went. Very difficult lady to resist was your Granny. Mind you, being nudged up the bum by Big V was a powerful incentive."

"Did she really make acorn and nettle wine?"

"Yes, but it was an acquired taste, like a lot of her wine. For my money, Granny Bidsmead's carrot and cauliflower wine tasted like the washing-up water after a curry meal. It was one I always tried to avoid."

I shuddered. "I always avoided all of them. Granny was great but she was no vintner."

"Big V liked them though."

"Yes, she did. Remember that old stone kitchen sink…"

"Ah, yes, strategically placed under Big V's oak tree and there was always a bowl of homemade wine in it. I tell you that vulture was a lush."

"But Granny's wine never did Big V any harm."

"Not on its own, no, but…"

Arthur's voice tailed off and I raised an eyebrow.

"You think someone tampered with it?"

"I do. Can't prove it, of course, not then, not now, but I think someone deliberately spiked Big V's wine."

"If we can't get the old lady, we'll get her vulture?"

"Exactly."

"Do you think they meant to kill her?"

Arthur thought for a moment. "Probably not. My guess is that they wanted to distract Granny but they couldn't have foreseen things happening the way they did."

"Suppose not, but it still makes them responsible."

My mind went back to that terrible day and although it was all very distressing I've always been glad that I was there for my grandmother when the crisis hit.

I shouldn't really have been there. I was on a three-day school trip to visit London museums but after the first day, I sneaked off and took the train to Copley to see Granny and Big V.

It was coming up to eleven in the morning and Granny and I were having a quiet cup of tea together when we heard a loud screech. We rushed outside and saw Big V lying on the ground, struggling to get up.

She saw Granny and began to make her way towards her. At first, she tried to fly but only got a few feet off the ground before flopping back down again. The most frightening thing was the noise she was making and we suddenly realised she had the hiccups.

"What's wrong with her," I cried.

Granny peered into the stone sink under Big V's tree and sniffed.

"She's drunk," she said grimly. "that ought to be my parsnip and oakleaf wine in there but there's definitely a smell of whiskey and rum too, if I'm not mistaken."

I had a sniff and reeled back. I never have liked spirits.

"How could that happen?" I asked. Oh, the innocence of a teenager.

"Give you three guesses," muttered Granny.

We gazed at Big V with a mixture of anger and sadness. She was a sorry sight – a bedraggled vulture with a glazed look and a violent attack of the hiccups. As we watched she managed to lurch to her feet and then, presumably obeying all avian instincts in times of distress, attempted to take off. She fell twice and Granny moved forward to try and help her but finally, Big V managed to get airborne. She just missed hitting the stone sink then executed a tight turn as she struggled to gain height and headed towards the road. Her flight seemed undulating and uncontrolled.

Parked by the gate was a huge JCB and with an effort Big V managed to gain enough height to pass over the top of it but suddenly, a massive attack of hiccups made her stall and she plummeted downwards. The JCB driver saw her coming and leapt out of the way. Unfortunately, as he did so he took his foot off the brake and the JCB began lumbering forward. Big V, still hiccupping wildly, landed in the driver's seat and must have hit another lever as the arm of the JCB rose into the air as the speed of the vehicle increased.

We suddenly saw it was headed straight towards a large bulldozer. The bulldozer driver realised his danger and abandoned ship as the JCB hit it sideways on. Neither vehicle was seriously damaged but they were both deflected so they were heading straight towards Number 13.

At this point, the speed of the JCB increased considerably. Later we wondered if Big V had collapsed onto the accelerator pedal but whatever the reason, before anyone could do anything about it, the JCB had crashed through Granny's garden fence, roared across the lawn and buried itself in the front room window. The window gave way against this unprovoked attack, the lintel crashed down on top of Big V and the whole front wall of the house began to sag.

At the same time, the bulldozer went through the glass conservatory like a knife through butter and took out the whole of the east wall.

Granny rushed across to the JCB calling for Big V but she was too late. The falling lintel had hit Big V full on the head and she was now a very dead vulture. Granny let out a scream of rage and turned back towards the house as the JCB, relieved of both driver and vulture, spun on a sixpence and, accelerating forward, demolished the kitchen extension. I saw what was about to happen so I ran forwards and grabbed Granny, dragging out her of the way just as the whole front wall of the house collapsed in a pile of bricks and dust.

Big V had achieved what the Council and the Law had failed to do but at a terrible cost.

Arthur came good on his original promise and a luxury room was found for Granny Bidsmead in a local care home but it was no good, the heart had gone out of her and she only lived for another three months.

There was an enquiry, of course, but it was a complete whitewash. It's virtually impossible for individuals to win against Councils, especially as Granny was technically in the wrong by refusing to comply with a compulsory purchase order. Had she been killed it might have been a different story but a dead vulture counted for nothing.

But we got our revenge, after a fashion. Arthur and I managed to rescue Big V's corpse and while the ramps to the arterial road were being constructed we snuck in there one night and buried the remains of Big V in the concrete. A pyrrhic victory of course but we get a secret pleasure from knowing that motorists accessing the main highway do so over the corpse of a much loved Lappet-Faced Vulture.

And there's one other thing which no one has yet noticed. I had a memorial plaque made up and, again in the dead of night, I fixed it under one of the pillars supporting the road. Strictly illegal, of course, but I doubt many local councillors potter around under the main road very often.

And I know it's there which is what matters.

In memory of Granny Bidsmead and Big V who fought the local council together and lost. Forever remembered.